Totally Bound Publishing books by Kady Ellis

Collections
Hot Bite: The Enemy of Her Enemy

I0663102

Hot Bite

THE ENEMY
OF HER ENEMY

KADY ELLIS

The Enemy of Her Enemy
ISBN # 978-1-80250-552-8
©Copyright Kady Ellis 2023
Cover Art by Kelly Martin ©Copyright July 2023
Interior text design by Claire Siemaszkiewicz
Totally Bound Publishing

Published in 2023 by Totally Bound Publishing, United Kingdom.

Totally Bound Publishing is an imprint of Totally Entwined Group Limited.

THE ENEMY OF HER ENEMY

Chapter One

Roan Silverthorne

Beneath my skin, my pelt itched. The city lights blurred the horizon and clouded the stars, leaving my inner wolf confused and antsy. I rubbed a hand over the center of my chest to soothe it as I stared at the hazy sky. Without the starlight to guide us, we were lost — or as close to lost as we could be in this age of cell phones and built-in GPS.

Of course, I'd made us all leave our cell phones back in the car outside the city, so the leeches couldn't track us. Much like the beast inside me, I didn't trust technology — though, unlike my wolf, I at least understood it.

The wolf understood that Polaris always meant north, that Orion's sword would lead him south. He knew the sun rose in the east and a scent mark would guide him home. Drop him in a strange forest and he'd be home before dinner.

A city, though…? He knew nothing of cities.

Luckily for my wolf, he was not a wild beast roaming free. Even if I thought of him as a separate being, as other—an animal spirit bound to mine by Mother Moon before she sent us to the earth as a babe—we lived together in harmony. His choices were mine, and mine were his, a true blending of consciouses in one body.

Behind me, my brother Micah, the pack beta, and Deacon, the pack bursar, were both just as twitchy, growling at shadows and flinching with every half-heard noise.

"I hate the fucking city," Micah grumbled as we took yet another wrong turn and ended up in a dead-end alley. "Tell me again, Roan. *Why* couldn't we have waited until the sun was up?"

"Because that's when the leeches will expect us to get here," I snapped back, spinning on my heels to start searching for the right street *again.* I'd booked the hotel under my omega mother's last name, one she'd abandoned after marrying my father, so it was unlikely the vamps would be keeping tabs on it. I had even printed directions to the hotel out before leaving the pack lands, just in case the leeches were tracking my phone.

I might be paranoid, but it had kept me alive longer than many of my brethren.

Of course, I hadn't expected *someone* to get carsick and throw up on the map. The reminder—of both the loss of directions and the sour odor we'd been forced to drive with—had me glaring at my brother again, who just smiled sweetly back at me. I *knew* he knew why I was glaring, just like he *knew* that look was always enough to get him out of trouble.

Fucking doe-eyed motherfucker.

"Can we at least stop for breakfast? We've been walking for hours," Micah whined.

"Twenty minutes, you big baby," I huffed, but since my own belly was grumbling, I kept my eyes open for a diner as we walked. It was the only good thing about cities, that they had places like that—ones that stayed open all hours of the night. The pack kitchen closed by nine o'clock sharp, except on Mondays. No one opened on Mondays.

"I factored four meals into the budget," Deacon answered, a hopeful note in his voice. "If we stay away from any of those fancy places and the leeches feed us like they promised, we can swing breakfast."

"Oh, hold your horses. I'm already lookin'," I replied, finally spotting the neon lights glowing at the next corner. Compared to some of the other shuttered restaurants we'd passed, this one looked ratty. The glass was yellowed and frosty with age, paint chipping off the doorhandle—*who bothers to paint a doorhandle?*— and the floor was sticky under the soles of my shoes.

But the air smelled inviting, of bacon and grease and burnt coffee—just like home, with less of the wet-dog stink. The door closed with a rattle and Micah pushed past me, heading straight for the table by the jukebox, the lights blinking. "Dude! It still works!"

Honestly, I was surprised he even knew what it was.

I rolled my eyes as I watched the pup dig through his pockets for stray quarters. "Think he'll ever grow up?" I asked Deacon, though inwardly I was glad my younger brother was less jaded than I was.

"You'll be sad when he does," Deacon answered, patting my shoulder as he strolled over to the booth and dropped. He grabbed a menu and skimmed through it. I supposed he was right.

"So, still hate the city?" I teased my brother as I sat across from Deacon and dragged out my own menu. A quick glance told me all I needed to know. *Steak and eggs, available all day every day.*

"Can we get a jukebox back home?" Micah asked instead of admitting he might like *some* things here.

"Sure. When you get a job that pays well enough to buy one," I agreed. He made decent money as my beta, but he blew through it as fast as he earned it, between his comic book collection and his chew toys.

"*Oooor*," he said, giving me a big smile, "my super nice, super rich boss could just me a raise."

"Yeah, sure. As soon as you start actually working instead of spending your days *working* your way through the guards' beds." I lifted a brow, grinning when he blushed.

"You...you know about th-that?" he asked with a stutter.

"Hard not to when you stumble out of the barracks half-dressed at nearly noon reeking of wolf pheromones, brother dear." Not that I judged him. At his age, I'd been just the same, except I'd been working my way through the women's quarters just as often as the men's. I was lucky I didn't have half a dozen pups out there calling me da.

Micah pouted. "Maybe I was sparring."

"Whatever you want to call it. I didn't ask, so...you don't need to tell. In the future, though, I would prefer you to keep your extracurriculars to *outside* of working hours." I winked at him just as the waitress strolled up.

She was rail thin, her nose chapped and red, her scent acrid, but she was polite enough as she smiled. "What can I get you fellas to drink? Soda, coffee?"

"Just water, ma'am," I answered for all of us. The fizziness of pop didn't sit well on our bellies, and if I had to smell either of them drinking the coffee, I was going to vomit.

"Oh, ma'am?" She fluttered her eyelashes. "My, aren't *you* a gentleman. I'll have those right up for you."

"Dude..." Micah leaned across the counter and swatted my arm. "Stop flirting. *You're* the one who said to keep our 'extracurriculars' outside of working hours!"

I leaned back in the booth, propping my right ankle up on my left knee and folding my hands behind my head. "What can I say? I'm a Casanova."

"You're a *dog*, that's what you are! And a downright hypocrite!" Micah pouted.

"Do as I say, not as I do." I grinned, accepting my water from the waitress with a wink when she returned. If I wasn't mistaken — and I rarely was — she'd undone another button while she was in the back, leaving a few more inches of pale cleavage on display.

I wasn't really in the mood to flirt seriously. It was more to tease my brother, and I felt guilty that I might have led her on. I straightened and tried to look more serious, thinking of the upcoming meeting with the leeches. If they didn't hold such a tight monopoly on the beverage distribution market up and down the whole coast, I wouldn't bother taking the risk.

She must have sensed the shift in my mood because her smile dimmed, and her voice turned more professional. "Are y'all ready to order, then?"

"Steak and eggs for me," I answered immediately, tucking away my sticky menu and downing my water. "And a refill, please."

"And for you, darlin'?" She turned to Micah, flashing her blue eyes again. Poor thing didn't realize she had the wrong equipment, but Micah didn't seem to notice her attentions, regardless. He was still frowning at me.

"I'll have the waffles, with extra strawberries. Oh, and extra cream, too, please."

"You're going to get fat," I warned, grimacing at the thought of that much sugar. "You should have some protein."

Micah rolled his eyes, "Yes, *Dad.*"

"Oh, cut the dear some slack. He's skin and bones," the waitress twittered, looking like she was just dying to pinch his cheeks.

Micah glared at her, and she backed off, scurrying away without Deacon's order.

"Just my luck," Deacon grumbled, throwing his menu to the side. "I guess I'll be right back."

"Order me a side of bacon while you're up there," I hollered after him. He replied with his middle finger.

* * * *

The sky was just starting to gray when we practically rolled out of the diner, patting our full bellies and groaning. "Good food," Deacon said, yawning. "Now, bed."

"Yes, bed," Micah agreed, snuggling up against Deacon with a yawn of his own.

I stared between the two of them, thoughtful. To my knowledge, Deacon had never dated a man. Though, now that I thought about it, I wasn't sure he'd ever dated *anyone*. I didn't think anyone was good enough for my brother, but I supposed if he had to end up with anyone, Deacon wouldn't be a terrible choice.

Before I could speculate too much, though, I froze, my nostrils flaring. My inner wolf clawed at my ribcage like a caged beast, howling at me to *pay attention*. To what, though? I spun on my heels, teeth bared in a growl as I struggled to figure out what scent he'd caught. Danger? Food?

I must have taken too long to figure it out because the wolf took control of my throat. Unused to this body, the single word came out strangled and forced...but still understandable. *"Mate."*

I followed the scent.

Chapter Two

Andromeda Dianus

The shadow moved.

For over ten blocks, it stalked me, skirting along the shallow curb of the uneven sidewalk. I might not have noticed it—this late at night, it was little more than a patch of deeper dark—if it hadn't grown so bold at the last crosswalk. It stretched long, oil-slick tentacles out like fingers into the yellow beams of a passing taxi's headlights. The stench of burnt toast filled the air as the shadow hissed, then it scuttled, spiderlike, backward.

I almost felt guilty, watching it huddle by the base of the dented trash can like a terrified feline, but the poor thing wasn't truly injured. While none of our historians could definitively say where the creatures came from, they all agreed they couldn't feel pain. Hearing it whimper and whine, I wasn't so sure.

I steeled my spine and turned away. I'd fallen for their little tricks before, when I was younger. I didn't have time tonight, not when I already knew what it wanted. It was unfortunate that it finally found me. I thought I'd gotten lucky when I snuck out of the Sanctuary undetected at witching hour and even luckier when I'd made it to the Golden Brew.

For the first time in almost a year, I ordered fresh herbs — sea holly, peony, calendula, nettle and rosehips — to make a new batch of daylight salve for the rest of the coven, the ones not blessed, if it could be called that, with being sunkissed, like me. The shop was even going to deliver them for me. With any luck, I'd have time to get them hidden before any of Arlow's minions pilfered them for her.

Even when she was on a different continent, she somehow managed to mess with my stuff.

All I had left to do was get to the bookstore as it opened. I'd parted with my favorite copy of Anne Rice's *The Witcher* — a signed first edition hand-delivered by one of our feeders — to convince the owner to break his rules and open the shop before dawn. A half-hour was all the time he'd give me. As a former feeder, even if he was from a different coven, the man knew of the things that went bump in the night. I was lucky he was giving me this chance at all.

A glance at the sky showed it graying into pre-dawn. A half-hour was just enough time for me to get to the shop, grab the book and flee. Any longer and I'd be trapped until sunset, or until my father sent thralls with a daylight carriage. I hated the vile things.

The other vampires, the *normal* ones, would end up with a few surface burns as they sprinted from the safety of the shadows to the pitch-black, airtight boxes — little bigger than coffins and just as uncomfortable. By the time they made it safely back to the Sanctuary, they'd be basically healed — maybe a little red, a stinging, itchy rash to remind them to not cut it so close next time.

Sunlight wouldn't kill me. It wouldn't even pinken my skin, not any more than it would a human's, anyway.

It would, however, send me spiraling into a frenetic heat, tormented by arousal until I sated it with sex or the sun set, whichever happened first. In my youth, I'd slept with more people than I cared to admit to, the desire for sex too overwhelming to ignore. As I'd matured, though, so had my self-control.

Now, I *could* choose to suffer through the cramping and unbearable horniness—but I'd rather avoid it. If I was quick, I should make it home in time. I was almost there. The shadow could wait a bit longer.

My father, apparently, disagreed.

I'd barely passed through the next pool of light when a second, larger shadow oozed out of the gutter before unfurling. Then, it stretched, its edges shivering.

I cursed and stumbled to a halt, barely avoiding stepping on the little thing. It didn't seem to care when I crossed my arms and glared down at it. The stupid thing just rolled forward to rub against my ankle through the thick, black boots.

"Shoo," I muttered, trying to nudge it to the side with my foot, but it refused to budge. Instead, it started vibrating in what could only be called a purr. "Come on. Scat. I don't have time for this."

I really didn't. A glance at my watch had me grimacing as I realized how close I was cutting it. My half-hour had already started.

But the little shadow was insistent, climbing up on me and clinging to my jeans with what felt like hundreds of little hooks, *whining* at me in a strange, pitiful cry. It was sharp and piercing, loud enough that

I feared it would wake the Blanks sleeping in the nearby apartments.

"Shhh!" I tried to quiet it, but the thing only grew louder. The creatures couldn't speak on their own — though they were near perfect mimics — but that didn't stop them from getting their point across.

Clearly, the thing had no intention of letting me keep moving, and trying to fight free would be worse than useless. "Fine. I said *fine*! Let go, and I'll let you deliver your little message. Come on..." Leaning down, I helped it unlatch itself.

The shadow squirmed as it landed on the sidewalk, excited as a puppy. I tried to ignore it as it yipped, but I'd always found the little creatures...oddly fascinating. A diaphanous mass of undulating dusk with little more than a slit at the apex... The mouth — if it could be called that — opened to an even darker abyss.

The voice that came out of it was sharp and far too familiar, Dad's anger evident even through the messenger. "*Come home.*" Two words, nothing more.

Not that the Vampire King would ever dream he'd need more. Dianus was older than dirt and had left a trail of bodies in his wake too innumerable to count.

I couldn't think of many vampires willing to ignore him.

For several moments, I considered it. It might be worth the lecture — even the disappointment I'd have to see on his face for *months* — to get my hands on the rare grimoire. It had belonged to one of the oldest witch families. I'd honestly assumed — like most people — that it had perished in the fire that had killed its owners.

I might never get another chance like this. It wasn't every day a witch line ended, especially one as powerful as the Briars.

I'd be willing to face King Dianus' entire army of thralls *and* his guilt trip.

But, then the second shadow joined the first, merging into a larger, even creepier being. The command that it repeated was loud enough to make me cringe and rub my ears. "*Now*, Andromeda."

Gah.

I was already under house arrest for no better reason then my father's paranoia. The last time I'd disobeyed him like this, he'd confined me to my rooms, as well. Six months of cold meals delivered from the kitchens and seeing no one but the thralls had epically sucked.

The Shadow quivered as the words faded in the night air, then flattened out, scuttling into the street before disappearing down a manhole. Even if I wanted to send a message back, it would be pointless. The buggers were hard to catch twice. One-way communication... They were — more message-in-a-bottle than cell phone.

Magical things, cell phones... Well, not *really* magical. If they were, then maybe I'd actually be able to use them. The damn things went on the fritz every time I so much as looked at them.

One of the Shadows slid a tentacle out of the manhole again, like it was considering repeating its message if I lingered any longer. "I'm *going*!" I yelled, and it disappeared back down the drain with a little *eep*.

"Just one night," I muttered, kicking at the sidewalk before turning around. "Was that too much to ask?"

I started trudging back toward the Sanctuary, grateful for the thick soles of my boots. The odds of finding a cab this time of night were slim — and a safe one basically a miracle. Not that any would-be mugger scared me... It'd take more than a measly human to be a danger.

But if Dad had to send out the cleaners, I'd *really* be in trouble. I took as long as I could to reach the Sanctuary—which was to say, a whole ten minutes. It was long enough for the enforcers to be waiting, impatient and antsy. They kept skirting their gazes toward the lightening sky as they dragged the iron gates open, waving me inside.

Chapter Three

Roan Silverthorne

I lost the scent outside what was clearly a witch-owned shop called the Golden Brew. The smell of too many herbs clogged my nostrils until I sneezed, then sneezed again. And again... Then Deacon and Micah started sneezing, and I broke down, jogging up a few blocks until I could no longer smell anything, my eyes watering.

My wolf growled inside me, but I shoved him back. *We don't need a mate*, I told him, annoyed when he kept pushing. It wasn't like I hadn't tried, even if a mate was the last thing we needed right now. Silverthorne Moonshine was taking off, and the more our name got out, the more wolves had started arriving, pleading to join.

The pack was growing so fast that we couldn't keep up with the housing. Some families had started doubling up, and we still had three camping in the main packhouse. I'd given up my own quarters for a family who'd just had a new litter while traveling, so even I was camping in the grand hall.

Ignoring his whining, I glared at the nearest street sign. "Is it just me, or is that it?" I asked, surprised that our accidental side trip may have actually gotten us where we were going.

"Holy shit!" Micah hurried ahead with a laugh. I rolled my eyes as Deacon and I followed. Before we reached the hotel — I could see the sign in the distance — my keen hearing picked up on the word 'vampire' from inside the bookshop we were passing.

Instinctively, I slowed to a stop and peered through the window. An older gentleman in a blue checkered sweater vest was carrying a heavy-looking book with antique binding toward a spiral staircase near the back of the shop. I could hear him grumbling as he walked, "...vampires playing pranks. Like I don't have better things to do with my morning."

Whatever the book was, if a vampire wanted it, that meant *I* wanted it...especially if it inconvenienced one of them. I turned away from the hotel and pushed open the shop door.

"Can I see that?" I called before the man could reach the stairs.

He turned with a frown that brightened to a smile when he saw me. "Ah, yes, sir. Interested in mythology, are we?"

"I just love old books," I said, instead of agreeing, hoping that sounding a bit naïve about what it was. A closer look showed clearly that it was a grimoire...and a real one at that. Stumbling on one like this was more than just *luck*. It was fate.

Owning a grimoire like *this* could be just the thing to draw in a Witches Circle. Our pack desperately needed wards for the boundaries and spells to purify the water we drank. Even a single witch could elevate our pack to the next level, if only we had something to offer.

With this grimoire, we'd finally have it.

Twenty minutes and a stiff negotiation later, I left the bookshop with the grimoire, carefully wrapped in protective leather wrappings, tucked under my arm. My personal bank account might be a few zeros smaller, but it would be worth it. I knew Deacon would argue that the cost should have come from the pack accounts, but I didn't feel right about that.

Our finances were strained already, what with building the new houses and having so many new mouths to feed. Pulling from that fund made me feel like I was taking food from a pup's mouth.

Deacon and Micah were waiting outside the hotel for me—one patiently, the other less so. Deacon just gave the package a curious look, but my brother, of course, tried to grab for it. A deep growl spilled from my chest as my wolf surfaced unexpectedly, oddly protective of the grimoire, and Micah flinched back.

"Jeez, I'll leave it alone. What is it, the holy grail?" Micah whined.

"No," I said, then cleared my throat when the word came out gruffer than I intended. "Sorry. It's a grimoire, for the pack."

"Ah," Micah immediately cheered up, accepting my explanation at face value. An Alpha was always protective of his pack and its property, so I supposed that could explain my wolf's irritation, but it felt like more.

"Let's go inside," I said, changing the subject before my wolf could get any more out of my control. It wasn't even the full moon, only a waning gibbous. There was no excuse for my behavior.

Micah went inside with no questions, but Deacon gave me a searching look before he followed him in, clearly sensing the same oddness I was. I just shrugged, unable to explain it. Something about the book had my wolf on edge. It could just be lingering magic residue, could be the abandoned scent of my mate.

Whatever it was, I just hoped he calmed down before the meeting with the leeches, because that was going to be tense enough already without managing my wolf's temper on top of it.

"Oh, cool! Dude, there's a toilet! And a *bathtub!*" Micah hollered a few seconds after we checked into our room, while Deacon and I were still unlacing our motorcycle boots.

"As much as this room cost, there better be," Deacon replied dryly.

"Dibs on the bed!" Micah hollered out.

"You can have the floor if you don't want to share," I raised my voice as I replied so he could hear me over the running tub. "And *don't* use all the hot water!"

"Too late!" he replied, far too chipper for someone aiming to get his ears boxed.

"I'll go babysit the pup." Deacon clapped my shoulder before strolling into the bathroom. A moment later, I heard him yelp then water splashing on tile.

Shaking my head, I flopped back on the bed. Before I could do anything but close my eyes and sigh, a sopping wet wolf the size of a shaggy Great Dane came barreling out of the bathroom, flinging drops of dirty water and clumps of fur in all directions. He took a running leap for the bed, one of his large, saucer-sized paws landing square on my chest and using it as a springboard to get to the pillows.

The breath was forced from my body with a grunt, and I barely resisted the urge to curse at my little brother, but I knew it would just lead to him slobbering my face in wet wolf kisses to apologize.

Micah curled up at the head of the bed, his tongue lolling out of his mouth. Two seconds later, a drenched Deacon came sliding out of the bathroom, nearly slipping on the wet tile floor.

"Micah!" He screeched, his face beet red. "This hotel has a strict no-pets policy!"

Micah's wolf—a brindled beast with thick, unruly fur and chocolate brown eyes, just thumped his tail twice on the mattress before rolling to his back, exposing his tan stomach. My brother was a slut for belly rubs.

He did not, however, shift back.

It was Deacon's turn to give me puppy-dog eyes. "Alpha...make him turn back. The deposit alone..." He groaned, likely at the thought of forfeiting it. There was a reason he made such a good bursar, always thinking of the purse strings.

I just shrugged, gesturing at the room. I knew my brother too well to think that I could get him to do anything if he had his mind set. "I mean, look around. The damage is done already." It wasn't a lie. The white rug had muddy footprints tracked across it, clumps of fur floated like dust mites with each blast of the air conditioner and that wasn't even considering the now-drenched, formerly white coverlet.

Deacon groaned. "We're fucked."

"Or at least our deposit is," I agreed, then rolled onto my feet with a groan. "And with that in mind, I see no reason the two of us should be stuck smelling wet dog all night while the mutt enjoys himself. Might as well join him."

So, I started to strip, piling my road-dusty clothing and the travel backpack we stored it in while we were shifted onto the fancy cream armchair by the window, ignoring Deacon's wince.

I breathed deeply as I stepped into the shift, letting my wolf uncurl. Before I could exhale, he was free, and together we fell forward onto our paws. We shook out our pelt and yawned. It felt good to stretch.

For a moment, our separate beings danced around each other in playful greeting, before they mingled again and we became one.

It wasn't so much of a leap as a step up onto the tall, king-sized bed. I nipped at my younger brother, who gave a brief whine before he conceded, moving farther down the bed and leaving me the soft pillows.

I circled them twice before I found the right spot and flopped down with a sigh, resting my head on my paws as I blinked toward Deacon. He'd give in soon, I knew it.

Lost deposit or not, even Deacon couldn't resist a puppy pile.

I was right. Indecision wavered on his face, warring with envy, before he sighed and gave in. He folded his clothes much more meticulously than I had, before he allowed himself to shift. His wolf, unlike mine and my brother's much larger dire wolves, was much closer in size to our wild brethren that we occasionally ran with back home. Except for the single white paw, he was entirely black.

Deacon sniffed along the foot of the bed before he finally leapt up to join us, the move graceful and restrained. I barely felt the mattress shift as he landed. He curled up near the edge, tucking his tail under his muzzle.

I didn't think it was my imagination that a moment later, my brother — in a little scooting movement that I suspect was supposed to be sneaky — wiggled on his belly until he was cuddled, as best he could be, against the smaller wolf. He tucked his nose against Deacon's side. Inwardly, I smiled at the unexpected sight.

In human form, Deacon was a large man with broad shoulders and a beard more befitting a lumberjack than a bursar. Micah, on the other hand, was slender and petite. At twenty-four, there were days he hardly looked older than a teenager. In *these* forms, though, the size difference was reversed, but the personalities hadn't changed.

I yawned, pushing away my curiosity, then wagged my tail with happiness. I was with pack. I was happy. Tomorrow—or later today, at this point—might bring stress and tension, but for now, in this moment, everything was as it should be.

Chapter Four

Andromeda Dianus

I was barely inside, the gates still clanking shut behind me, when it started.

"He's waiting in the throne room," the taller of the two, a dark-haired vampire with the gray skin of the freshly turned, said.

"Where else would he be?" I muttered but didn't wait for an answer—nor did I waste time going up to my room to change. If he wanted to see me immediately, he could accept me arriving in less-than-appropriate dress.

He should be used to it by now, anyway. In the three hundred years since his concubine had birthed me, I'd not once been described as 'elegant' or 'refined'. The closest I'd ever gotten was when one of my father's old friends had called me a 'bluestocking' during a dinner party. He'd meant it as an insult, but I found it fetching.

Of course, my father turned blue in the face when I spent the next thirty years requisitioning actual blue stockings from the tailor to wear. For some reason, Father thought it 'uncouth'. My mother, until she'd died a scant few years later, found it charming.

At the time, I hadn't thought much of it, but since her death I'd begun to suspect that my mother had felt trapped by her life. The youngest of King Zacharius of House Karayan's eight daughters, she had been gifted to my father as a token of peace. And, until her death, the treaty had been successful.

As expected, my father just gave my outfit—dark-wash jeans and black tank top under my favorite studded leather jacket—a shake of his head. He was dressed in a suit tailored by our coven's exclusive designer. The dark crimson fabric was threaded with rubies and diamonds, as befitted his status. I had a dress upstairs that matched, though I'd never worn it.

Father moved on. "Welcome home, Daughter. You know, home…the place you have been forbidden to leave, *especially* without your enforcers, and yet…"

Dad waved a hand toward the pair of vampires kneeling to the side of the throne, their arms behind their backs and heads bowed. I could smell their blood—jasmine and plum, but sweeter—and I knew without looking they'd been lashed.

"Hardly fair, Father," I said as I crossed my arms, anger filling my chest. He knew I hated when he did that, punished the thralls for my behavior. "They're practically infants. You can't expect them to be a challenge if I seek to leave."

"I *expect* them to do their jobs, just as I expect *you* to follow my rules." He didn't even need to raise his voice. I could hear his disappointment, sharp as broken glass.

I cringed before I convinced my spine to straighten. "Dad, I'm not a fledgling anymore. Those rules—"

He interrupted me, slamming his fist so hard on the obsidian armrest that the whole throne shattered into gravel that spilled across the marble floor, rolling like dice in every direction.

Father landed on his butt, dust clinging to his suit. A look of shock appeared on his face, and I couldn't help the giggle that slipped free before I could contain it. I slapped my hand over my mouth, but not in time. Dad's face twisted and the witchlights flickered with his anger.

"Enough!" Father stood and brushed the dirt from his pants, distaste pulling at his lips. Immediately, several thralls rushed in from the shadows with push-brooms, scrambling like ants to start clearing away the evidence of the king's outburst. One of them approached Father with a lint roller, but Dad's glare sent him scurrying away.

Father met my eyes again. "Those rules are there for *your* protection, Andromeda. Every day, the Ainwicks circle the Parliament like rabid dogs, fighting for any scrap of power they can wrest away from us, the Karayans, the Ardeleens... Yet our allies grow thinner with each waxing moon and our enemies thrive. Have you forgotten your mother's fate?"

My body jerked and I cringed, dropping my gaze to the floor. It was a low blow. It had been me who had found her body in her bedroom, broken like a porcelain doll...shattered. They'd never found her killer, though most of the Lords blamed the Lycans—except for the Karayans, who blamed my father.

I could still see the shredded skin on her neck...smell the faint scent of plum when I closed my eyes. Like the Karayans, I too suspected the killer was someone much closer to home, though *I* knew better than to suspect my father. He'd loved her dearly, and her loss had nearly killed him.

"I'm sorry," Father finally said, breaking the painful silence. "But, my precious child, how I worry. You are the only thing I have left...of her." His words seemed to catch in his throat, filling me with guilt.

I knew that my next words would only make me feel worse, but he needed to hear them. "Mother was killed in our own Sanctuary, in her own bed. Her enforcers couldn't protect her then, and I'm no safer now, whether I stay locked away like a damsel in my tower or live my life."

The king's eyes burned red, anger drawing his power close to the surface. "You are careless, child. I will *not* attend to your corpse, just so you can traipse around the city on a whim. Especially not now that the Lycans have been stirring—"

"Lycans?" I didn't mean to laugh, but the idea was ludicrous. "They're practically extinct! The only pack close enough to even worry about is the...what? Silverthornes? Last I heard, those swamp wolves have an Alpha who is barely more than a pup and a handful of runts. Besides, since when do they come into the city?" They'd purchased a large tract of land some years ago from the Joyce Wildlife Management Area in secret and had, according to rumor, built their own little village on the little bit of land that wasn't a swamp. Last I heard, they didn't even have running water.

"Since their distillery started gaining a following and they need a new distributor for their moonshine, a representative of the pack will be meeting me tomorrow, just after noon. I expect you to keep your guards close and avoid the throne room."

"Is it still a throne room when you don't have a throne?" I blurted without thinking, staring at the bit of gravel that was all that remained.

Dad huffed, his shadow stretching along the marble as he stepped off the dais to stand in front of me, tall and regal. "Remember who you are and what you stand for."

"Barely more than a figurehead," I answered, refusing to bend to his...fearmongering, "in a coven that now doesn't have a throne." I smiled brightly at him, truly hoping that he would see the humor in at least one of my jokes and forget about the lecture I knew was coming. If that didn't work, maybe I should throw in some flattery. "There isn't a vampire alive strong enough to challenge you."

"Are you willing to bet the lives of every vampire in this kingdom on it?" Dad countered, no hint of a joke on his face. "I have only three heirs, Andromeda. If not you, who am I left with?" Dad stepped even closer, looming over me until my shoulders hunched and I tipped my neck, acknowledging his power.

Dad didn't stop with my submission, and his words hit me harder than if he'd struck me. "Tell me, Daughter. On whose head should I place my crown? Arsenious?" Dad scoffed, though pain lurked in his eyes. "Almost two hundred years and he's still locked in bloodlust. Will he rule our kingdom with compassion?"

I barely remembered the Arsenious of my childhood. I'd been barely out of nappies when he'd succumbed, only days before my mother had died. Our historians claimed it a common thing as a vampire aged, particularly those who'd been turned— something about the human brain and how our venom reacted to it. One could be perfectly fine for decades, centuries, then it would hit without warning.

A vampire in bloodlust wanted two things and two things only — to feed and to fuck. They would walk into pure sunlight if they caught a scent they liked, no care for the consequence, and their strength was boundless. Poor Arsenious had destroyed more cages in the dungeon than they could count.

I knew the real Arsenious was in there, somewhere. I'd done a dozen Dreamwalks, and in them I could feel the edges of sanity — brief moments of consciousness interspersed with the ravings. It was painful to see, and I didn't know if my efforts were helping, but for my father's sake, I couldn't stop trying.

He'd wake from it someday, the historians claimed, though lately, even they had seemed skeptical. I could hear it in their voices when my father asked about him, though *his* voice was always filled with hope.

Arsenious had been my father's champion during the Lycan Uprisings. His strength and valor were still spoken of in hushed tones, in shadowed corners after dinner parties. Before he'd succumbed, no one would have dared challenge my father, not with Arsenious at his side. Of King Dianus' three heirs, only Arsenious had earned the title in battle.

I'd been given mine by right of birth. As I was my father's only naturally born offspring, the title was mine by blood and bone. The third heir, though...

As if he could read my mind, my father's eyes narrowed. "Or would you prefer Arlow?"

I cringed at the mention of her name, just like my father had known I would. She was nothing more than a spoiled brat playing princess. Her sole occupation seemed to be draining father's bank accounts as fast as she could.

"Arlow can stay in Florence or wherever the hell you sent her on vacation this time," I blurted, my skin flushing with anger.

Father gave me a knowing look as his words did exactly what he'd intended—reminded me why I couldn't do the things I wanted without consequence.

Arlow—or Low, as everyone but my father called her—was the whore my father had taken as a lover after my mother's death. At first, I'd thought my distaste for the woman was simply the knowledge that she was my mother's replacement. After all, the last thing I'd wanted while my mother's body was still warm in her casket was my dad's new *hole* trying to tell me what to do. To make up for my unkind inner thoughts, I'd tried so hard to be kind. When the vampires in our Court snubbed her, I'd rallied to her defense.

Unfortunately, the Court had been right.

Arlow was nothing more than a former feeder turned harlot and gold-digger. She'd admitted to my face—and had the audacity to say it in *front* of my father—that she'd only let him turn her in the first place because she knew what his bank account looked like.

The poor little fool had been operating—mistakenly--under the misconception that being sired by the king would make her the queen. Oh, the temper tantrum she'd thrown when my father had laughed.

It made her a potential heir, nothing more. Our queens were born, not made. We hadn't had one in longer than I'd been alive. Every generation of vampires was born with the *potential*. It took the right combination of magic and circumstances for the potential to blossom.

Any other woman would have been happy with the luxury apartment, fancy clothes and monthly allowance bigger than the GDP of a small country and gifted vacations to lavish resorts like candy…but not Arlow.

She had the audacity to be *offended*, walking around like a peacock with her nose in the air as if we'd stolen something from her. When she was away, my dad could admit that possibly, he'd chosen poorly. I thanked the stars every evening that the harlot was off moon-bathing on a beach somewhere far away from us.

Dad's mouth twisted, and my heart skipped a beat.

"No…tell me you didn't…" I groaned.

It was Dad's turn to look guilty. "She's actually home for the summer."

My stomach dropped to the floor. "You have *got* to be shitting me."

Dad didn't answer. Instead, a voice from behind me made me cringe. "Aw, aren't you happy to see your step-mommy?"

I'm going to kill her.

I wanted to vomit as I watched my dad's eyes soften, the harsh line of his mouth pulling up to almost a smile. I knew it was bio-chemistry — the sire-bond was impossible to break, short of dying, and would flood the sire with endorphins at the mere sight of their bonded.

It didn't make it any less disgusting. I could probably have handled seeing my father look at someone like that if the expression was directed at literally anyone else. Unfortunately, unlike Arlow —

who lifted her skirts for any vampire who shot her half a glance—my dad was loyal.

Lecture forgotten to the call of his bonded, Dad's attention focused fully on Low. He had the eyes of a starving man at a feast—hungry and needy. Arlow shot me a smug look as she sashayed past me. Her outfit was skimpy—better suited to a streetwalker than one of my father's heirs—and my nose wrinkled at the stench of drying semen.

"Were the showers broken?" I muttered angrily as I glared at her.

She just winked. "Run along, kiddo. Daddy and I have babies to make."

Shuddering at that gross thought, I backed out of the throne room. Before I could slam the door shut behind me, Father gave me one last order. "Go directly to your tower, Andromedas, and I expect you to *stay* there until I say otherwise."

I slammed the door behind me, barely resisting the urge to holler, "Whatever!" I pitied the poor thralls stuck inside, forced to watch me. As I walked up the staircase to my tower apartment, though, I couldn't help but chuckle.

It appeared that, despite the sire-bond, my father had managed to keep *some* things from her. Surely, she should have questioned the lack of a child by now, as often as she spread her legs?

Turned vampires were infertile, frozen at whatever stage they were in when they were turned...which meant their eggs were, too. Most of the time, I felt bad for them, and...if I were honest with myself, a bit guilty as well. I had a perfectly good uterus with no intention of putting it to use, not for a few more centuries anyway.

Arlow, though? Yeah…no guilt there. I hated to think what kind of trauma her kid would end up with. She'd be lucky if it survived to adulthood. I'd be worried she'd forget the poor thing in a limo somewhere, and it would end up gods knew where.

If she didn't smother it with her inflated ego.

I closed myself in my apartment with a sigh and flopped down, fully clothed on my bed. After a few moments, I kicked off my boots and toed my socks off, flinging them toward the hamper.

While I was grateful that Arlow couldn't have any kids to neglect and traumatize, I couldn't help but wonder what it would be like to have a sibling.

It got lonely up here in my tower.

Maybe that was why I did it… I'd certainly failed often enough to know it was pointless. A waste of ingredients that would be better served as daylight salves and sleeping potions for the Elders.

But they were my ingredients to waste.

I left my bedroom and moved to my conservatory. There, I gathered the dried rosemary — fresh would be better, but I could only work with what I had — the henbane and mandrake, grinding them to dust in my stone pestle. I set the powder aside while I examined my belladonna, picking the best three of the blackberries and adding them to the pestle.

With my mortar, I began to smash them, mixing the juices with the powder until it formed a thick, dark paste. I didn't bother grinding the moonflower. I picked three petals and carried them with the pestle into the kitchenette. It was the work of only moments to get the kettle on. The moonflower petals went into the water to steep, then I added the paste to the bottom of my favorite teacup, the one I only used for Dreamwalking.

I didn't care how good the dishwasher allegedly was. If I was taking a stomach tonic, I didn't want to accidentally end up walking around in my dad's dreams. Because...gross.

Soon, the kettle started screaming, and I removed it from heat, carefully adding the moon tea to the cup. A dash of honey and a quick stir later, I was carrying it with me into the bedroom.

The tea, as always, made me gag. The sweetness of the belladonna berries and honey wasn't enough to counteract the bitterness of the moonflower or the rotted flesh taste of the henbane, and I didn't think there was anything strong enough to block the odor. I'd made the mistake of adding sugar once.

Never again... I still had nightmares about it.

The effects were quick. I didn't even have time to set aside the teacup. Instead, it fell to the carpet as I dropped back on the mattress. My blue coverlet threatened to swallow me. The ceiling above me started swimming, stretching down like white-fingered gloves — then I was sinking.

Chapter Five

Arsenious Dianus

Hunger bit my belly, tore into it like a ravenous dog. I gnashed my teeth, flashing fangs, but the silver muzzle clamped around my jaw kept me from feeding, made my words little more than animalistic growls.

I could smell them, hear them...even *see* them, their humanoid bodies as they lurked by my pen door. I can't reach them. No matter how hard I strained against the chains, they refused to break.

"Are you s-sure, l-lady?" a cowardly, quivering voice stammered. *Male. Thin, hardly more than a mouthful.* Not worth the effort—or wouldn't be, if the hunger wasn't tearing me apart. *Her,* though? She had curves and swells and though she had no smell—neither of them did—I knew how she'd taste. She would sate the hunger in my belly *and* the one in my loins.

Her pale hair hid her face, but I'd take her from behind before tearing out her throat. Her looks were meaningless. All that mattered was the taste.

"I don't care of the risk, just do it." The woman's voice was whiny. My growls grew louder to drown her out, but she moved too quickly for me to register, then pain flared along my side.

For the first time, I noticed the strange, black stick in her hand. It had two points at the end, not sharp enough to be daggers, but when they touched my body, it shocked me. I screamed and tried to pull away.

A *lightning* stick.

She gave me a nasty smile as my voice choked off.

"We've given him so much already..." The male said, his voice pleading. Cowardly he was, the way he sniveled by her side, the fear in his gaze as they met mine.

"Obviously," she said, rolling her eyes. There was a falseness to her smile as she placed her hand on the man's cheek. "Our plan wouldn't have worked with him in our way, would it?"

"Can't you just kill him?" He whimpered and I grinned, even through my muzzle.

I'd love to see him try. Deep, *deep* inside of me, a sentience stirred, reminding me of the years we'd spent in battle, the weight of a sword in our hands and blood in our bellies.

"You know we can't, darling. After my dear husband passes, we'll need him. Imagine the horror, the tragedy. Poor little Andy found in her bed, murdered just like her mother, and Arsenious the killer? The Council will have no choice but to name me queen." The woman's smile looked as crazy as I felt.

But then the weakling came closer, jabbing a needle in my arm, and I screamed again as the hunger grew stronger tenfold. Whatever awareness I'd had of the room faded to the pain. The sentience died, drowning as the hunger swallowed it.

Chapter Six

Roan Silverthorne

I am walking down an endless, narrow tunnel. The walls are white stone, too perfect to be real. When I stretch out my fingers, I see them touch but feel nothing, only air. Something nudges my thigh and when I look down, I see a large, black wolf.

He looks at me with a mix of pity and contempt, then nips at my thigh again, his teeth digging into my flesh — why am I naked? — as he pulls me toward the other end of the tunnel. I give in to his demand and start walking. Despite my nudity, it is neither cold nor hot. There is no smell, despite the wind that seems to be trying to push me back.

When I slow, though, the wolf grabs for my hand, dragging me on. It should hurt, the way his teeth sink into flesh, but when he releases me, my skin is whole and unmarred.

We walk and walk, but the walls stay the same. I feel like I'm on a treadmill going nowhere, until suddenly, we reach a stone door that wasn't there a moment before.

I look down to ask the wolf if we should go in, but he's gone. I am alone.

I open the door.

Inside is a bedroom. At first, it is empty. The furniture is there-not-there, solid as smoke rings. It ripples like the surface of a puddle until I step inside and everything snaps to stillness.

The room is no longer empty.

The bed is covered in a rumpled blue coverlet, pillows a mess, and atop it, a redheaded woman is sprawled. One leg dangles, the foot bare, to the stained carpet. A teacup rests on its side, half hidden under the bedframe.

The woman is not pretty.

She has hair like a flame but it's a knotted halo around her pale face. Her nose is too long to be pert but too short to be regal, her cheekbones just a bit too sharp. I would have passed her on the street if we'd met on the sidewalk, but there is something vulnerable about her that has me stepping closer.

Her lashes flutter, her eyes darting quickly from side to side.

Another step closer. I reach toward her, pulled inexorably forward. I can't stop it – but then a hand grips my wrist.

A man with crazed eyes and wild blond hair is standing beside me, and it's his hand that restrains me. I try to pull free, but his grip tightens.

"Help her." His mouth doesn't move but I hear his words clear as day.

Before I can ask why or how, I wake up.

Chapter Seven

Roan Silverthorne

The Dianus Coven was housed in one of the oldest privately owned buildings in New Orleans, a mansion that resembled a church in form but not coloring. The stone was dark, and even in the summer heat gave off a chill. It must save thousands of dollars in cooling costs, especially in this heat. Particularly since I knew, like most supernaturals, that the vampire covens were stuck in the dark ages—quite literally, since most modern technology wouldn't work around them. Something about their magic and the way it interacted with the electrical fields, I'd guessed.

To me, the fact that they didn't have computers or cell phones didn't mean they had to ignore the modern ideas of democracy and free will. While they were no longer allowed to enslave other species, that didn't stop them from keeping thralls of their own.

A deplorable practice. The sooner we could get out of the city and back home, the more comfortable I would be. The gates closed behind us, and now I felt trapped. I couldn't help the way my gaze skirted along the iron bars, searching for weakness—looking for a way out.

Beside me, Deacon cleared his throat, and the sound reminded me of where we were and how my perusal might look to the vampires watching us like hawks. I plastered on a smile. "King Dianus is expecting us."

I meant it as a question, but I couldn't keep enough growl from my throat to make it anything but a demand.

"Right this way," the vampire said with a sniff, turning his nose up.

"Dog," the other vampire muttered, anger in his voice. Perhaps the other guard didn't realize how keen our hearing was—or maybe he just didn't care. It was all I could do to ignore it.

I did, however, take note of his face, just in case we ever met in a dark alley in the future. Our species might be at peace now, but I knew, like we all did, that it could change at any moment. Better to know the ones already set against us.

The first vampire—or at least I thought it was the first, as they all looked the same to me—led us into the vampire Sanctuary. The ceilings in the entryway were high, and the walls, despite the stereotypes, were lined with elegant, jewel-studded mirrors. I grimaced as I caught our reflection in the glass.

Even in our nicest clothes, we looked out of place. I didn't own a suit or tie and neither did anyone else in my pack. We had the funds now to buy them but not without stretching our finances more than I'd like. For now, it was mid-summer. Game was easy to hunt, and our gardens grew lush and bountiful. No one went to bed hungry. Soon, though, the summer would fade to fall and into winter. I couldn't stop thinking of the lean months coming.

Our hunters were stocking the deep freezers with as much venison and rabbit meat as they could spare, and two of the younger wolves, just barely out of their parents' dens, had worked hard through the last winter and spring to get a greenhouse started. I was hopeful that this year, winter would go easy.

At least there were supermarkets now, only half-a-day's drive away, so the risk of true starvation no longer loomed over our heads like a hangman's noose. Instead, we only risked financial ruin. We needed this deal if we hoped to keep our profits growing as fast as our pack was.

I ran a hand down the front of my nicest shirt, a red gingham button down, feeling the buttons catch on the palm of my hand, then I tugged on the collar of my leather jacket. "Should have bought new pants," I muttered, frowning at my dark-wash jeans.

"If the way we dress prevents them from seeing the benefits of this deal, then they're too stupid to be valuable partners anyway," my younger brother said, loud enough that his voice echoed against the stone. I swallowed a laugh. Thankfully, our vampire guide stayed silent.

"You look fine, Alpha," Deacon promised.

"The king is waiting for you," our guide eventually said, hovering outside a set of thick black double doors.

"Thank you for showing us the way." The apology burned my lips. Everything inside me rebelled against being polite to one of *them*.

I might have been born after the Wolves' Revolution, but barely. My father had been fresh from the battlefield when my mother conceived me. I will never forget how angry his scars looked — the red, inflamed bites that ringed his neck like a collar. For fifty years, they'd lingered, only barely silver when he'd finally passed too young. At not even two hundred, he should have had a century more, at least.

I gathered every shred of dignity I had around me and straightened my spine as the vampire pulled open the right door and held it. Asking the leeches for help went against every fiber of my being. For my pack, though, I would do it.

The servant on the other side gave me a sneer, his nose wrinkling as he took a step back, but at least he announced us without embellishment. "Alpha Roan Silverthorne of the Silverthorne pack and his betas, Micah Silverthorne and Deacon Carrick to see King Dianus."

"Enter," King Dianus permitted. His voice was loud but cold, echoing against the high-domed ceiling. I was ten feet into the throne room before I noticed that the Vampire King was sitting, not on a throne, but in a red brocade upholstered armchair.

It was not the image I expected, but something about that had my shoulders relaxing. It seemed the vampire wasn't as stuck in the old ways as I'd heard. If the rumors truly were wrong, perhaps our partnership might not be so bad.

King Dianus stood from the armchair and descended the dais, waving regally toward a conference table set up to the side. It was strangely modern and too shiny *not* to be new. At the head of the table a manila folder, an open notebook and fountain pen and a ledger that looked to be filled with numbers waited in a neat stack. A tubby vampire with cheeks that almost had color in them stood awkwardly behind a chair just to one side. On the other, a pretty woman with eyes like a shark was already sitting, doodling in the margins of a spiral-bound notebook.

"Have a seat." Dianus gestured across the table as he sat down.

I felt awkward as I took the chair at the other end, my back to the throne room door. Deacon and Micah sat only a heartbeat after I did.

"Shall we get started?"

Two hours later, we'd hammered out all but the last few details. King Dianus demanded exclusive distribution rights nationwide, but I was willing only to guarantee it across Louisiana — but we were making progress, until the door opened behind me and that scent — that same alluring, *intoxicating* scent my wolf caught yesterday — filled the throne room.

My wolf woke. "Mate," he snarled, and I spun, my gaze landing on a redheaded woman with fire in her eyes.

Chapter Eight

Andromeda Dianus

"You...you want me to leave the Sanctuary?" The girl's eyes were wide as she backed up against my dresser, her skin paler than it should be. I hadn't taken much, barely more than a handful of swallows. A feeder of her size shouldn't have even noticed the loss, so I knew the paleness was from fear.

"I mean, yes? It's not like I'm asking you to go to the other side of the country or anything. I just want you to take a cab to the bookstore and give the owner a letter," I said with a frown, not sure I understood her reluctance.

"But...but it's daytime!" she yelped, and her whole body shuddered.

"Uh...yeah. That's why I'm asking *you* to do it?" Jeez, was the girl dense? A human, especially one that worked *here*, should be more afraid of the dark than daytime. They had firsthand knowledge of what kind of monsters lurked in the night.

The curvy woman dropped to her knees, shaking her head and *literally* crying. "No, no...no, please don't make me. I *can't...*"

Frowning, I stepped closer, squinting my eyes. Out of the shadow of my feeding couch, did she look a bit...gray?

With a growl, I grabbed the collar of her shirt and yanked it down, exposing more of her shoulder. There, by her collarbone, a faded pink mark... "What have you done?"

"I...I don't understand..."

Unfortunately, I knew she was lying.

"You know the rules. *Two* feedings per week, that's it—never more than two. So, I'll ask again... What have you *done?*" My words grew quieter but were no less sharp as I stepped closer, barely able to restrain myself from shaking her.

"I... She... It was a lot of money..." She finally broke down and admitted, wringing her hands. I could tell she wanted to shove me free, but even in the midst of turning, she was smarter than that.

Still, I released her and stepped back, shaking my head. "How many other vampires have fed on you this week? Just the one?" For her sake, I hoped so. It would be a messy transition, but if only one vampire's venom was battling mine in her system, she might still survive.

She nodded, but something about her expression told me she was lying again.

I should have asked her to deliver my message first, then I'd have seen it immediately. There was only one main reason a human would be so terrified of the daylight. It was instinctive, and one of the earliest symptoms of the vampire virus overpowering the human's immune system.

"I don't believe you. Was it *only one?*" I asked again, deepening my voice.

Slowly, she shook her head, fear growing on her face, but I wasn't naïve enough to think she understood her situation. Likely, she was expecting punishment for breaking the rules — but the rules were in place for *their* safety, not ours.

"You silly little fool," I muttered, pity seeping from my voice.

"Am…am I in trouble?" Fear flooded her face. She jerked forward before catching herself. "Am I going to get fired?"

"Oh honey, no. No, you're not going to get fired." I stepped forward and wrapped her in a tight hug as my heart broke.

No, the truth was so much worse.

Moving so quickly that she wouldn't even notice, I let her go and clasped her head in my hands, twisting sharply to snap her neck. She died instantly, but tears burned my eyes.

She didn't deserve this.

But it was the most humane way.

She could never have survived the transition. Too many different venoms fighting for dominance in her veins, none of them strong enough… I'd seen it before, once. A feeder had been selling information to a rival house, and my father had decided to punish him.

He'd had seven vampire Lords bite the man over the course of a week, and the man had died in agony. The venom had literally eaten him from the inside out. By the end, he'd looked like a leper, and I'd never forget his screams.

I'd find out which of my brethren had fed from her, and they *would* be punished. Since we tracked who drank from which feeders and when, it wouldn't even be that hard. All I had to do was cast a *Hindsight* spell on the mirror in the corner with a few drops of her blood, and I could watch her through the past week, clear as a reflection. Then, I could compare their names to the authorized list.

By noon, I had a list of three vampires and a strong desire for vengeance. That poor girl was *barely* forty, far too young to die. She should have had decades left...maybe a century, if she stayed a feeder long enough. Our venom, even in doses too small to cause a turning, could repair enough small damage to prolong a human's life.

What happened to her was so far from necessary that there was no way to justify it. Those three vampires had no excuses, and I didn't even bother tracking them down to ask why. Why had they paid her under the table to break the rules? It wasn't like they were starving. We might not have as many feeders as we'd had a century ago, but a century ago, we hadn't had the artificial supplements we had now.

I stormed to the throne room, shoving past the thrall who tried to stop me. He wasn't willing to hold my arm tight enough to hold me back, which must mean he didn't *really* want me to stay out—or so I told myself. Dad was probably just screwing around with Arlow.

That's what I thought, anyway, until I remembered, too late, that my father was meeting the Lycans today. They sat—my father and his advisors on one end, the strangers on the other—around a conference table.

Whatever conversation they were in the middle of died on my entry. My father's enforcers immediately moved in synchrony to surround him, the sound of swords being drawn from sheathes ringing in the air.

My father had barely lifted his hand to wave them off when the three strangers stood, their growls loud and echoing. I only had eyes for one.

He had golden eyes, half wild as they met mine, and unlike the wolves at his side, he wasn't snarling. Instead, he looked startled and uttered a single word, "Mate."

Before I could even understand the word, the large Lycan appeared in front of me, almost like magic. I knew it wasn't, that he must have moved, but I was so tangled in his gaze I didn't notice. The strange Lycan stood more than a head taller than me with the shoulders of a linebacker. He could pick me up and break me before I could stop him, and suddenly, I understood my father's fear.

The Alpha—because there was no doubt in my mind whose shadow I was standing in—was bigger than anyone I'd ever met, but his size clearly had no impact on his speed. And *that* was in his two-legged form. I'd always assumed the paintings of Lycans in their *other* form were exaggerated.

Now, I wasn't so sure.

I swallowed, and the Alpha's golden eyes dropped to my mouth. Then, he leaned in, his breath hot on my skin. My heart rate sped up, but not with fear. Arousal swirled in my belly as I inhaled his scent—an intoxicating wildness.

It grew stronger as he leaned in close enough that the tip of his nose brushed the skin of my neck. The small part of my mind that remained rational was quickly overpowered by the more primitive monster that lived under my skin, the one that urged me to tip my neck farther back and submit.

It was a familiar feeling, this sudden need that filled me. I'd felt like this the few times I'd been caught out in the sun, a reckless lust that tried to convince me to spread my thighs and beg.

I barely had time to process the feeling — let alone shove it down — before several of my father's enforcers were dragging the Alpha back. He twisted his lips in a snarl as they forced him away. His fingernails started to lengthen and darken into claws before he curled them into fists, hiding them from sight.

His broad shoulders lifted in a visible inhale before he forcibly unclenched his jaw. Then, my father stepped between us, blocking my view. His back was tense and stiff, his voice angry as he spoke. "Take your mutts and go. This meeting is over."

"King Dianus, I assure you... The terms of our deal —" one of the other Lycans, smaller by a fraction then the Alpha — which wasn't saying much, considering his size — said, lifting a hand placatingly.

"Out! There will be no deal, Roan Silverthorne! If one of your kind so much as *looks* at my daughter again, we will be negotiating *war*, not distribution rights!" My father bellowed loud enough that even I cringed.

"Father, I think —" I started to interrupt, embarrassed at his overreaction. The Alpha certainly hadn't hurt me. If anything, he'd done the opposite, if the dampness between my thighs meant anything.

Not that I'd *ever* admit out loud that the big man made me want to fall to my knees for him. I was the heir to the throne, and that came with *expectations*. Being submissive had never been one of them.

"Darling." This time it was Arlow who spoke, her voice wheedling, and there was something cunning in her eyes that had me immediately on edge as she glanced at me. "I'm sure he meant no harm. Besides, Andy's a big girl. You don't *really* want to give up the chance of being the *only* distributor of Silverthorne Moonshine, do you? Not after losing that mead account… Oh…what was it? Wintermead?"

Arlow might have sounded naïve to someone who didn't know her, but *I* heard the edge to her voice. Very few people knew Wintermead had pulled their product from the Dianus Company. Arlow shouldn't have even been one of them, though I wasn't surprised that she had her nose digging around in the business. After all, she lived on money and gossip.

Losing that account had been a big hit to our bottom line. One we could sustain, certainly, but the sooner we replaced it, the better all around.

I stepped to the side and saw the look on the Alpha's face. It hadn't taken Roan long to come to the same conclusion Arlow had, not if his expression was any guess. Whatever bargaining power my father had coming in to the meeting was gone now. We needed Silverthorne brewery much more than they needed us.

And my father knew it, too. From the fury on his face, he'd been planning on sending the Lycans away now but likely reaching out in a few weeks, after they'd had time to stew over the lost contract. Now, they'd be sitting around waiting in expectation, not fear.

For the first time I could remember, my father cursed, going so far as to raise his voice at Arlow and me both. "Out! To your rooms, the both of you! I'll deal with you at dusk."

I couldn't help giving the Alpha one last, confused look before I started for the door. Unlike Arlow, I knew better than to argue. Father wasn't going to change his mind this time.

I was in the hallway, the door not quite closed behind me, when I heard my father yell, "Enough! Out of my sight!" A smirk crossed my mouth and I slowed, waiting to hear Arlow get yelled at again, but I was disappointed.

She came barreling out behind me with a loud huff, nearly tripping over her heels as she tried to elbow past me. Rolling my eyes, I didn't bother trying to stop her. She could be in as much of a hurry as she liked. With the sun in the sky, there was nowhere to go. She clearly chose *not* to go to her room—she'd turned the wrong way—but I didn't bother to follow. Whatever she was getting up to was her business, and Dad could deal with it.

I wasn't her babysitter or her warden. The Sanctuary was plenty large, but there was only so much trouble she could cause, and *none* of it was my problem.

Besides, I had my own things to worry about. My attempt at using Dreamwalking to wake Arsenious last night had failed—again. I still had to tell my father about the situation in the feeding room. And somehow, I had to find a way to get a message to the bookstore.

Chapter Nine

Andromeda Dianus

It took longer to track down the three vampires than I expected, considering there were only so many places in the Sanctuary to look. By the time we found all three and the enforcers had them in daylight cuffs, dusk was long passed, and I knew my father would be pissed when I showed up at my room.

Maybe that was why I decided to stall. Instead of going back upstairs, I wandered farther into the dungeon. No matter how much I tried to claim otherwise, even if only to myself, I wasn't moving aimlessly. I ended up standing outside the twelve-inch-thick Lucite glass that kept Arsenious safe — and us safe from him.

He couldn't hear me. The room was soundproofed, and the filtration system kept him from catching any stray scents to fixate on. The guards who brought in the blood bags and force-fed them to him wore scent suppressants to lower their risk.

They were paid well and above the going rate, regardless. We'd lost at least one a decade when Arsenious had figured out a new way to escape whatever supposedly unbreakable cage we had him in.

Now, he was lying on the thin blanket that substituted for a bed, his eyes closed but body still twitchy. I don't move or speak, but somehow, he still sensed my presence. Quick as lightning, he was on his feet and standing in front of me, only a foot of plexiglass between his face and mine.

There was no recognition in his face as he started hitting the glass over and over. I could feel the way it vibrated with every strike. Nervous, I waited for a telltale crack that didn't come.

Over and over, he struck it, his face twisted in a growl, until his hands were bleeding, violet blood streaking down the glass like a rainstorm. I swallowed down my tears at seeing him like this and turned away, leaving him — and the other prisoners — behind.

My skin was cold as I ascended the stairs to my tower, my gaze lowered to the marble of the steps. At first, I didn't see my father waiting, I only saw the silver wingtips of his shoes. I raised my eyes slowly until I saw his face, then I winced.

He was livid, his jaw clenched hard enough I could see the muscle twitching. "Funny," Dad said, crossing his arms. "I wasn't aware that your bedroom had moved."

"It hasn't," I replied, though I knew what he really meant. Why was I coming upstairs now when I shouldn't have been out of my bedroom in the first place? "Are you coming in?" I said as I skirted around him, holding the door.

He followed me inside, his presence making the room seem smaller. I watched him walk to the windows and push aside the curtains, staring down at the gardens through the special UV-treated glass. His back was stiff and the room silent. I didn't dare to even fidget.

"This was your mother's room," Dad said abruptly, letting the curtain fall but not turning around, "when she first came to live with me."

"I...I didn't know that," I said, surprised. I'd always thought that she moved right into my father's quarters.

"She loved looking down at the gardens. She said that even if —" Dad's voice broke off in a laugh, but it wasn't pleasant. It was sharp and filled with pain. I watched his shoulders move as he drew in a ragged breath. "She said that even if she had to be in a cage, at least it was a pretty one."

I flinched hard at the words. They echoed my own feelings too closely. "I didn't realize..."

"Why would you?" Dad turned from the window, the skin of his face pulled tight. He looked drawn. "She loved you, Andromeda. She only smiled when you were in the room...called you her perfect little princess."

"I don't hate this room," I blurted, worried he'd brought it up because he thought I felt imprisoned as well. Sometimes, I did. Sometimes, I paced the floors like a caged animal, desperate for freedom. But most of the time, I understood that Dad was scared.

Dad sighed. "You're so much like her, Andromeda. Just as...headstrong, independent." Dad grimaced and rubbed his chest, his voice strained. "She would..." Dad coughed, swaying slightly.

I jerked forward with my hand stretched to steady him, but he waved me off. "She would have loved you."

"Dad!" I screamed as he fell to his knees, his skin going ashen. I dropped beside him, cradling his head in my hands. "Guards!" I hollered, but silence was my only answer. Quickly, I examined my father's face and hands, trying to stay calm enough to evaluate him.

His skin was gray, and a pinkish-white foam started dribbling out of the corner of his mouth. Poison, surely, but which one? I pulled back on his eyelids, noting the narrow pupils, then felt his skin. He was chilly, almost like ice.

I couldn't be certain, but I was guessing either juniper or mayflower, though I couldn't rule out holly. I could only think of one thing to do without more time to prepare. I jerked to my feet and ran to the conservatory, working as quickly as I could to grab the materials. I knocked over half a dozen jars before I had what I needed.

Roots of the belladonna plant, acacia and rose petals, a hunk of charcoal I normally used for sketching and honey. Grinding them together to a paste seemed to take forever, and I cursed myself for not having replaced my bezoars after the last batch of daylight salve I'd made.

Without knowing exactly what he'd been dosed with, it was hard to make an antidote. I just had to hope for the best. I ran back to my bedroom and dropped to my knees beside my father. He was still—too still, though I could hear his heart beating.

I had time, but not much.

With my fingers, I scooped as much of the paste from the stone bowl as I could and shoved it in my father's mouth, trying to get him to swallow. He had just taken in a ragged gasp of air, his eyes opening but glazed, when I finally heard the thundering of the guards' footsteps coming up the stairs.

But unfortunately, they didn't come in alone.

Arlow swept into the room behind them, dressed in mourning black. *Why is she dressed in mourning black?*

Her scarlet lips were painted in a frown, but her eyes... Her eyes were swimming with glee. "Guards," she drawled, "arrest the princess for treason. She poisoned my dear husband."

Chapter Ten

Arsenious Dianus

"You idiot!" The blonde woman whose name I didn't know was snarling, pacing my cage but never getting close enough for me to grab. "How did they get away?"

"I'm sorry, my love," a weasel-faced vampire cowered from the woman. "No one could have expected her to run, let alone send him to the earth..."

"Of course she was going to run, you idiot! I accused her of treason! What did you and your men think she was just going to do, sit there and *cry*?" The blonde slapped the back of the man's head.

"Well, yes. I mean, she's just a girl..." Weasel whined. The woman slapped him again, hard enough that his dark hair flopped into his face.

I yanked on my shackles. If I could just break *one* while they were distracted, I could be free, but they were still too strong. The hunger burned in my belly, but it felt subdued, waning for the first time in too long. My head felt filled with cotton.

"I am surrounded by imbeciles," Blondie said as she struck the weasel about the head a dozen times, until the man fell to his knees with a cry.

"Love, *please*... Even you didn't think she'd break the window!"

"Are you saying this is *my* fault?" Blondie's voice grew high and shrill enough to hurt my ears.

"No, no, of course not, of course not..." Weasel cringed back but Blondie just turned away, meeting my eyes for the first time.

She stepped closer with a frown. "You're sure he's still under?"

"Hm?" Weasel stayed on his knees for a second longer before he slowly straightened, pushing himself to his feet.

The sentience inside me swelled, and for once, I allowed it. Weasel leaned close — too close — to my face. *"Bite him,"* the sentience whispered to me. *"Fight."*

I snapped my jaws, narrowly missing him. He jerked back with a yelp.

"Careful, you moron. If he gets a taste of *you*, this whole thing is useless!" Blondie pulled Weasel farther away.

"He's...he's definitely still under," Weasel stammered.

"Good. Get him the scent, then let him go." Blondie turned on her heel and swished out.

"Wait! Arlow, wait! You want *me* to...to do it?" Weasel hollered after her. The woman didn't answer. I heard the man swallow as he turned toward me, approaching slowly. He fumbled, awkward and clumsy, with a bag made of a strange clear material —

like the bags they brought me blood in but flimsier. Something red was hidden inside.

The weasel finally tore it open, and the scent struck me like a hammer.

I snarled, straining against the shackles to get closer. I wanted it, and more than that I wanted the woman the scent belonged to. It was intoxicating, addictive…like the finest wine tempting an alcoholic.

The cowardly man pulled the fabric—a shirt, I realized—from the bag and waved it at me, nearly whipping me in the face with the cloth, but didn't bring it close enough for me to grab, not even with my teeth.

"There you go," the weasel murmured, slow like he was talking to a dog or an idiot. "Get the scent, yeah…"

I yanked harder on my chains. They clanged and jangled but didn't break.

"Can't believe I'm doing this…" the coward said, even quieter, as he pulled a brass key from his pocket. His hand shook as he skirted toward the side of me. I watched him with eyes like a hawk.

"If you want to get the bitch *this* belongs to"—he waved the red shirt—"you won't try to bite me or any of that shit, got it? Nod if you understand…"

After seconds of indecision, I finally nodded. He stepped closer, fumbling the key as he tried to put it in the hole in the shackle around my left ankle. I stayed still while he unshackled one foot, then the other. I even stayed still while he unlocked my left wrist, though it was hard. But, as soon as the last shackle fell to the cement floor, I lurched forward.

He tried to run toward the open cell door, but I was faster. A quick snap of his neck and his body went limp. *Drain him,* the sentience inside me said, sounding stronger than ever.

I was starving, so I agreed, swallowing the still-warm blood by the mouthful. There was no time to savor the taste—not that vampire blood tasted like much of anything anyway, but compared to the cold bags I'd been subsisting on, it was practically a feast.

I started for the stairs, but the sentience took control of my legs and stopped me. *No. The other way.*

I resisted his urging to find the back tunnel, the narrow escape route built just in case the Sanctuary was under attack. *How did he know of it? How did I?*

I shook my head, trying to clear it. I felt odd... Part of me wanted to ignore the voice and take the stairs, follow the intoxicating scent on the red blouse the weasel man had waved under my nose. Like a bull, I could take the stairs and kill anyone who got between the scent and me.

The sentience grew stronger, pushing against the feral thoughts. *No. That isn't who we are. This is a trap... Take the tunnel. We can find her that way,* it wheedled and coaxed.

Only the thought that we could still find her made me agree. "We'll try it your way," I growled to the sentience as I started following his silent directions deeper into the dungeon. "But when we find her, she's *mine.*"

Chapter Eleven

Andromeda Dianus

The three-story drop from my window to the lawn shouldn't have been a problem—and normally, it wasn't. I'd made the leap more times than I could count over the years—just never during the day and never carrying an extra two hundred pounds. But there was no way I was leaving my father behind for Arlow to finish off at her convenience.

Unfortunately, there weren't many places in the city I'd feel safe enough going alone in the state I was about to be in, let alone with the king of our coven in tow. And unlike me, Dad wasn't sunkissed. He wouldn't be left in an uncomfortable state of arousal after too much sunlight. He'd be left a charcoal briquette.

There were safehouses—several of them—available throughout the city, but the second I showed up at any of them, the coven would be alerted. Without knowing who we could trust, it was a risk I wasn't willing to take.

And I *definitely* couldn't show up at any of the other covens.

I knew what I had to do. I dragged my father along with me toward the garden, grateful he was still unconscious. The sun was already turning his skin bright red. Any longer out here and it would start charring.

I pulled him into the shadows of the willow tree before I laid him on the dirt. Already, I could hear yelling inside the Sanctuary, and I knew I was running out of time. "I'm sorry, Dad," I said as I grabbed a handful of dirt and quickly started drawing the runes of healing and protection on his face.

Then, I planted my hands on his chest and pressed.

The earth opened beneath him, roots shifting — writhing as they grasped at his clothing like fingers. I waited just long enough to watch the earth close over him before I fled.

I hated leaving him behind, even in the safety of Mother Earth's arms. He would stay in her embrace for an entire cycle of the moon, out of danger while he healed from whatever he'd been dosed with. If I hadn't found allies by then, though, he would emerge right back into danger — likely with no warning and no clue what he was walking into.

I raced through the gardens toward the back of the property, leaping the wrought-iron fence. The sound of guards flooding out of the Sanctuary onto the lawn grew louder as I landed. Ducking low, I skirted along the fencing until I reached the sidewalk of the main street.

Right would take me farther into the *Vieux Carre*, toward our safehouses, but my instincts were warning me away. I turned left, running until I no longer heard sounds of pursuit behind me. Even with the daylight salves, the sun would slow the guards down and be a drain on their energy. I knew my flight was drawing enough attention that even outpaced, they'd still be able to follow.

The sidewalks might not be as crowded as they would be closer to evening, but they were far from empty.

Heart pounding from adrenaline, not exertion, I forced myself to slow down to a less noticeable pace, hanging a sharp right at the nearest intersection in hopes of confusing my pursuers. Even walking at a slower pace, though, I was still on the receiving end of far too many stares.

It took me two more blocks to realize it was because I was barefoot. My skin was tough enough that I hadn't even noticed, but even in New Orleans, it was an odd sight. Thankfully, a little boutique on the next corner bent the rules and allowed me inside. I snagged a pair of socks and some new leather combat boots off the shelf, tearing off the tags and putting them on right there. They weren't as nice as the expensive, custom-made pair I had at home, but they would serve their purpose.

I carried the tags to the counter and passed over my credit card. If there was a way to avoid running it, I would have, since I knew that the charge would lead anyone looking right to the store. Unfortunately, I was going to need every bit of cash I had on me to get out of the city undetected. Better they traced me to here then to wherever I ended up.

The cashier, a girl with neon-pink hair who looked barely out of her teens, handed me my receipt with a forced smile. I reached out to take it, but before I could, I cried out as a cramp twisted my lower abdomen.

"Oh, fuck," I moaned, bending forward and clamping a hand over my belly. The sunlust was starting. I could feel the heat under my skin, tingling between my thighs.

"Are you okay?" the cashier asked, but I could see how her hand drifted below the counter, likely going for a panic button.

I nodded quickly — a lie, but she didn't need to know that — and grabbed the receipt, shoving it carelessly in my pocket. "Do you have a restroom?" I asked, desperate.

She popped her gum as she shook her head. "Not for customers."

"Not even for emergencies?" I pressed, clamping my thighs together as I tried not to squirm. If I could just take care of it now, I knew the first wave would pass quicker, giving me more time to get somewhere safe.

She shook her head again. "Nope. Soon as we let one person back, everyone'll have an 'emergency'." She made air quotes around the word.

"Thanks anyway, I guess," I grumbled, leaving the shop as quickly as I could. I was uncomfortable now, and it was only going to get worse. Everything ached, and I was no closer to coming up with a plan — no closer to coming, either.

A taxi rounded the corner and my heart leapt at the sight. Struggling toward the curb, I frantically waved my hand, attempting to flag it down. For a moment, I thought it was going to pass me by. At the last moment, it slowed to a stop, its brakes squealing. I yanked open the door and half collapsed into the backseat.

"You drunk?" The driver, a squat Cajun man with graying hair and thin-framed glasses, asked as he glared at me in the rearview mirror.

"*Alors pas. Allons!*" I snapped a rebuttal as I slammed the door shut, throwing on my own Cajun accent. It had been decades since I'd spoken it regularly, but I fell into it as easy as a well-worn pair of shoes.

"I'm not cleaning up vomit *bag daer,*" he *bouded,* but obediently stepped on the gas. "Where go, *cher*?"

"Just drive. I'll tell you where to, soon," I replied. *When I figure it out myself,* I added silently.

He shrugged and started to drive, peeling out into the street. He narrowly avoided clipping the front bumper of a trundling white van. Only once we were in motion did I allow myself to relax against the seat and draw in a ragged breath. All I wanted was to soothe the fire in my veins and loins, to shove my hands into my pants until I'd eased the kindling lust. Instead, I clenched my hands into fists and closed my eyes.

Immediately, a face swam behind my eyelids. Golden eyes and wild brown hair...

"Joyce WMA," I blurted. "Take me there."

For a moment, the cabbie fumbled with the wheel, glancing at me like I was a *couyan.* "You got the money for that?"

I yanked out my wallet—thank God I wasn't one of those women who insisted on lugging around a fancy purse or I'd be penniless--and waved it. "And a *lagniappe* for you if you get me there for dusk."

The cabbie stomped the gas pedal, and I jerked back at the sudden increase in speed. "You sure, *cher*?" he asked, though I could tell from the tone of his voice that he was hesitant to ask. "That bayou's been closed down to tours for nigh on ten years, you know…"

Of course it had. That was the whole reason I wanted to go there. The Silverthorne pack had bought it all official—though on the downlow, since most of the human government was unaware of our existence—and closed it to the public indefinitely for 'renovations'.

I didn't know if I was making a bad decision or a worse one, but I couldn't think of one better.

If Arlow hadn't poisoned my father directly, which was possible, since I'd never known her to lift a finger to do anything she didn't absolutely have to, she'd at the very least helped orchestrate it. Without knowing who helped her and who would help her again, I couldn't trust anyone—not the feeders, not the courtiers, not the thralls.

If I couldn't trust them, then I'd have to put my trust somewhere else…with the enemy of my enemy, the last place anyone would think to look.

I had to hope that the man who had called me 'mate' would be willing to help.

The memory of his golden eyes did nothing to cool the flames burning between my thighs. I clenched them together and swallowed my moans. I could feel my mind growing hazy, overcome with need. With any luck, the sunlust would fade before I ran into any of the Lycans.

"Lady. Hey, lady!" The cabbie smacked the leather seat in front of me, the sound jarring me from my drifting thoughts—thoughts of the Lycan's big hands and thick thighs, the way his shirt had stretched over broad shoulders. "I ain't sittin' here all day. Fare's one-fifty."

My hands were shaky as I pulled out my wallet again, throwing two Benjamins onto the front seat. They cabbie snagged them up quickly. "That's it?"

I growled, lifting my hand to the silver pendant I wore around my throat, and he lifted his in surrender. "No need for that. Keep your *gris-gris*, I's just asking."

The necklace held no magic, but I didn't bother correcting him. Mostly, I grabbed it to keep myself from grabbing *him*, but I wasn't too bothered by him backing down from it.

"Well? You getting down?" the cabbie asked and I realized we'd been sitting here in tense silence for at least two minutes.

I shoved my wallet back into my pocket and stumbled out of the cab. I'd barely closed the door when it peeled away, leaving behind nothing more than the stench of burning rubber. When he was out of sight, I finally turned to face the swamp.

I didn't care what anyone said, there was just something *wrong* with choosing to settle in the bayou. The Spanish moss might be pretty hanging from the cypress trees, but the water smelled stagnant and brackish, green clumps of algae drifting sluggishly along.

The old boardwalk still stood, though the wood was wet and partially rotted in places. A metal gate blocked it off from the road, faded signs warning trespassers to 'Keep Out'. *If only I could.*

The only thing worse than hiking into the swamp was hiking into the swamp like *this*. It would take a miracle on a good night for me to avoid stumbling around in circles, but trapped in sunlust? All I wanted was to walk back to town and find myself a one-night-stand or three.

"Focus, Andy," I said out loud, pinching my forearm in an attempt to stay lucid.

I couldn't just wander aimlessly. While I didn't *think* Arlow would realize where I was headed, eventually *someone* in the Court would get smart and hire a witch. One simple spell and it would lead right to me. Until I found a place to stop, I couldn't ward against it.

The protections required runes to be carved into living wood growing at each of the cardinal directions at points equidistant from the place I'd be sleeping. In other words...I'd need a place to sleep for the spell to work. If I had my potion bag or a better grimoire, I would have more flexibility, but as it was, the Look-Away Ward was going to be my best option.

Though, now that I was thinking of it, scrying might be a better option for me than continuing to wander aimlessly. I doubted the Lycans would have clearly marked signs leading to their village. If they were smart—which they were—they'd want to keep it hidden from any illiterate tourists who chose to ignore the giant signs at the beginning of the boardwalk.

Not to mention, I doubted even more that I'd be able to reach their village from the boardwalk in the first place. Lycans weren't known to shy away from dirt or marshes. There was no saying there would be a path to get there at all.

I might get lucky and catch their scent before one of them caught mine, and *maybe* I'd be able to track it back...but it would take time I might not have. And with the condition I was in, the longer it took, the more dangerous this whole endeavor would become.

I felt like I was seeing the world through fog, and my skin was hot and clammy, like I was running a fever. At least I was finally out of the sunlight, but the damage was done. My skin was flushed pink, and the world was swimming in a haze.

I was going to have to scry.

I *hated* scrying.

Potions, antidotes, salves…those were easy. With the right knowledge and combination of herbs, anyone could do it. Wards, spells, scrying…that was harder. I did better with magic that pulled from the earth. My species had always been more connected to her than most. Internal spells, like scrying, though…

Well, let's just say they didn't always go the way I planned.

Chapter Twelve

Roan Silverthorne

"Alpha! Alpha!" a young wolf—it took me a second to place his face—named Kaiyo hollered as he came skidding around the back of the packhouse, his hair a white halo around his head. He was one of our newest arrivals, a refugee from a pack out west. When the Westwood Alpha had died last year, no one had anticipated the bloody war that had broken out between his two sons and their supporters.

I'd taken in six families to date.

"Alpha! Zerek and I went hunting! Can we eat this? Zerek says yes, but it's so *creepy!*" Kaiyo asked.

Halfway through chopping firewood, I was lucky I didn't put the ax in my thigh, my head turned so quickly. I scoured his hands for whatever mystery thing they wanted to eat, my heart dropping to my knees. Zerek was born in our pack and *should* know what was safe to eat...but he was also an adolescent wolf, and they weren't known for making the best decisions.

I clapped my hand to my chest in relief when I realized he wasn't talking about a tarantula hawk, a coral snake or a pickerel frog, any of which would be poisonous enough we wouldn't make it to town. Instead, he was waving around a crawfish.

"*Don't* be eating things out of the bayou if you don't know what they are, boy," I growled as the fear started to recede. "This ain't your grandpappy's pond."

Kaiyo dropped his hands, lip sticking out in a pout that would make a puppy proud. "I wasn't eatin' it without *askin'*, Alpha…"

"Oh, stop all that *boudéin*. You just about gave me a heart attack," I said, but I couldn't resist the look. "Tell you what. How about I show you how to cook one?"

Kaiyo looked disappointed. "You gotta cook it?"

"Unless you want me to take you to the vet for an anti-parasitic." I narrowed my eyes as I issued the threat, hoping it would forestall the foolish youngster from trying it on his own.

Instead, he just looked queasy. "Uh…Zerek's been eating them since noon."

"Of course he has," I sighed. "Well, come on, let's go get the *couyon* looked at."

Zerek wasn't hard to find. I just followed the sound of horseplay. We lived on such a narrow tract of land that you could see one end of the village from the other. It made keeping track of the youth a less difficult endeavor. They still wandered off into the swamps if we turned our backs for too long, but unless they ran into a gator, our young could handle their own.

It was the poachers that worried me.

Our pack had settled in the center of the last remaining stand of uncut primary growth cypress trees, just off the north shore of Lake Pontchartrain. The ground here was solid enough to build on, and it was far enough from the trails that any too-brave — or too-*stupid* — hikers who chose to ignore the signs wouldn't stumble on us by accident. The limitations were worth it to keep us safe from the hunters who saw our second form and killed us for sport.

It'd cost a pretty penny for the filtration system that purified our drinking water, and we hadn't built attached bathrooms yet — though the kitchens all had running faucets. This time next year, all fifteen cabins and the packhouse would be fully functional. With the way refugees were flooding in, though, the number of houses would be quickly outpaced.

Zerek was older than Kaiyo and the other boys who surrounded him with wide eyes by more than a decade. He still had a few more to go before he'd reach maturity. We didn't consider our young fully grown until they hit at least forty. At nineteen, he was just now entering the awkward, gangly-legged years of puberty. The pups surrounding him still had faces full of puppy fat and impressionable minds.

I cuffed Zerek over the back of his head before he saw me coming. "Ow, hey!" he hollered, rubbing the area above his ear as he twisted around to glare at me — until he realized that it had been me who'd cuffed him.

Immediately, his eyes grew contrite. "Sorry, Alpha!"

"What's this I hear about you eating the crawfish?" I asked, refusing to be swayed by his innocent expression.

"I was just telling the boys — "

"You were just lookin' for trouble, that's what you were doing. Up you get. Hurry, now. I got other things to be doing." I snapped my fingers and his eyes widened.

"Oh, come on, Alpha! I wasn't doing no harm. Dad'll switch me if you tell him!" Zerek stuck his lip out in a wobbly pout.

"And you'll deserve it. Don't give me that *bouder*. But I doubt he'll switch you this time. A trip to the vet seems punishment enough, don't you think?" I lifted a brow as I said it, holding back my smile when his face twisted up in a horrified grimace.

"The *vet*? I'm not a dog, Alpha! It's not fair!"

"What's not *fair* is showing the little ones to eat something that could make them sick, which *you* will be if you don't get an anti-parasitic." I refused to back down on it. We were going. The only question was if he was walking on his own or I was carrying him.

"Can't I go to a human doctor this time? It's so...*embarrassing* at the vet."

"It's also half the price. If you think you can talk your dad into covering the cost of the doctor, then—"

"No!" Zerek interrupted and stood abruptly. "I'll go to the vet. Please don't tell my dad?"

I frowned at his back as he scurried toward one of the flat-bottomed pirogues waiting near the bank of the Tangipahoa River. We'd take the river all the way up to Lee's Landing, where the pack kept a few trucks to get us into town. I hesitated by the side of the boat as Zerek climbed in.

Something about the way he was so worried about his dad had me nervous. It was rare—extremely rare—in our society for a pup to be mistreated. Rare, but not impossible.

"Zerek, you know you can tell me if something's wrong, right? If you don't feel safe at home — "

Zerek interrupted me, "What? Oh, no, my dad don't hit me or nothing. Well, he took a switch to me that one time, but I guess gator-*wrassling* wasn't all that smart."

I cringed at the memory. Nothing quite stops your heart the way seeing a pup — in his two-legged form no less — rolling around in a swamp with a gator thrice his size and the pup poised to lose.

Zerek continued talking, pulling me out of the scary memory. "He's just going to get that disappointed look on his face, you know the one? And Mama will send me to dinner without dessert — and she's making King Cake!"

"Well, I hate to say it, Zerek," I said as I pushed the boat into the water and climbed in at the last second, "but by the time we get done at the vet, I don't think you'll feel much like eating anything."

"Aw, shoot."

* * * *

The vet in New Orleans was a nice, jovial man who promised he'd try to work my pet 'dog' in between clients as quickly as he could. He'd left me in the lobby with the parting words of, "Wow, look at him. Really takes after his ancestors, doesn't he?" before he headed into the back again.

I looped the handle of Zerek's leash — more for show than out of any actual necessity — around the arm of my chair and settled back. He was lying placidly on his belly between my feet. Every so often, I'd feel his body twitch as he caught the scent of an animal coming in or heard hinges squeal in the back, but for the most part, he was calm.

I yawned, the wide movement stretching my jaws until I felt them pop. I hadn't been sleeping well lately. With the latest influx of members, sleeping space was at a premium. I didn't regret giving up my bedroom to the young family, but my body liked to remind me I wasn't as young as I used to be. It needed more than a pillow and blanket on the wooden floor to be comfortable.

I let my head fall onto the back of the seat and closed my eyes. Surely a *little* nap while I waited wouldn't be too big of a deal...

I'm back in the bayou, on the boardwalk. Why am I on the boardwalk? We never use it. *Above me, the trees form a thick canopy, rays of light piercing like daggers. Something in me is warning me away from them, away from the sunlight. Faintly, I hear someone calling my name. It's distant but I know I need to follow it.*

I start to walk.

Inside me, my wolf is impatient, urging me to go faster. He nips at my sternum until I pick up my pace. I can tell I'm getting close. The voice is getting louder. It's a woman's voice, calling for help.

Calling for me.

I find her on a soft bed of moss at the base of a cypress tree — my mate, the Vampire King's daughter, the princess. Her red hair is tangled in a way that seems too real for a dream, her face flushed. She looks sunburned, her eyes glazed when they meet mine.

Her jeans are unbuttoned, riding low on her pale hips. "Alpha," *she moans and lifts her hands to cup her breasts. They are small but fill her palms just right.*

My own hands itch to take their place.

"Please, Alpha. I need." She spreads her thighs and the zipper of her jeans creeps lower, exposing another inch of flesh. *"Touch me, Alpha."*

I step closer. *It's just a dream… There's no harm in giving in.* I kneel on the bed of moss. It's soft and plush and feels so real that it's like I can smell it. I cup her knees, opening them wider until I can settle between them.

"Tell me you're mine," I find myself saying, the words emerging almost against my will. They are my wolf's words. He's a possessive beast.

"Yours," she agrees, arching her back. She lowers her hands to her jeans, slipping under the waistband to stroke the forbidden petals hidden between her thighs. I can smell her arousal, the heady musk. Before I can do anything, she looks to the side. "And his," she adds.

I turn my head and see a blond man. He's familiar, and I realize why almost immediately. He's the man from my dream, the other one…the one who told me to "Help her." Somehow, I doubt this is what he meant.

I growl at the thought of sharing her but realize quickly that the instinctive sound came from me, not my wolf. My wolf seems…calm — too calm for such a normally possessive beast. Silently, I ask him why.

"Ours," the wolf answers, but I can tell he's not just talking about the woman.

The blond man steps closer. His eyes are less wild now, though they hold the same glaze that hers do. "Ours," the stranger agrees before his eyes drop to her. "Alpha, she needs."

"Yes," she agrees, then she is shoving her jeans down in a fluid motion. She casts them aside and they land half in the swamp. I don't bother saving them. I'm too entranced with the smooth flesh of her thighs, the blushed lavender of her skin. Her slender fingers hide her silken folds from sight until she parts them, allowing us a brief, teasing peek.

"Touch her, Alpha," the stranger urges.

I trail my fingers up her thighs, tracing the lilac veins. She whimpers, her body quivering.

"Touch me, Alpha," she echoes, arching up into my hands.

It's just a dream, I remind myself as I strum the taut tendons at the apex of her thighs, scant inches from my destination. "That's mine to touch, naughty girl," I murmur, refusing to give in to her pleas – no matter how badly I want to – until she lifts her hands. She drops them to the moss beside her, curling them into little fists instead.

"Good girl," I purr my approval at her obedience. She might be a princess, but that doesn't mean she's in charge.

Especially not now, in my dream.

Here, she can be my submissive little pet, my good girl, my... "Pretty little kitten," I say as I finally allow myself to touch her, stroking the little nub above her slit until she cries out.

Beside me, the stranger – I wish I knew his name, though...does a man in your dreams need a name? – groans, his gaze locked on my hand as I pleasure her. "Take yourself out," I order him.

He does, and the thrill of knowing that he will submit to my will as well has my already hard dick throbbing in my jeans. "I want you to stroke yourself, but don't come." I watch him start to move his hand, the head of his dick – longer than mine, but thinner – a violent purple as it peeked out from his fist with each motion.

I turn my attention back to the woman. Her knuckles are white against the emerald moss, her head flung back to the bark of the cypress. And her mouth...the glistening pink lips are parted on a gasp. I can't resist. I slip two fingers into her core, relishing the wet heat that clamps down on them as I lean over her to capture her mouth with mine.

She tastes of cinnamon.

I plunder her with my fingers, curving to reach that spot — "There it is," I murmur as I find it, massaging it with my fingertips until she screams against my mouth. A gush of wetness coats my hand as she quivers, her thighs clamping down against my side with her climax.

"Come for me," I say against her lips, but my gaze is on his, the stranger. He groans, hand flying faster, until his seed coats the ground.

I woke up in the lobby of the veterinarian's office with a start, my heart pounding and dick pressing painfully into my zipper. Embarrassment flooded my cheeks as I spotted the damp spot darkening the front of my jeans. A quick glance around had me feeling grateful when it seemed no one else had noticed.

I swiped my hand over my face and sat up. There had been a distinct lack of privacy in the village lately. Apparently, I needed to take a few more 'runs' through the marshes if it meant I could avoid a situation like *this* happening again anytime soon.

Chapter Thirteen

Arsenious Dianus

"What the hell was that?" I blurted out as I jerked to my feet and back to awareness. For the first time in who knew how long, I finally felt fully myself, though that didn't explain the odd...dream — or whatever that was. There was something familiar about the powerful man who'd brought the redhead to orgasm, and something even more familiar about *her*, though I didn't have a name for either.

Hunger burned my belly at the thought of her, though not the same kind of hunger I'd been trapped in for far too long. I'd seen the slickness she'd left on the man's fingers as he touched her, and my mouth watered at the thought of tasting it.

"It's just a dream," I muttered, trying to put it out of my mind as I started walking again. These tunnels had been unused and abandoned for nearly as long as humans had walked the city above. My kind had built them to stay out of the daylight and only chance had kept the humans from stumbling on them.

My footsteps were nearly silent, muffled by the thick layer of dust on the stone ground. Elaborate spiderwebs threatened to entangle me. It would be easy to brush them away as I walked, but I'd rather leave as little evidence of my passing through as possible, just in case anyone tried to follow me.

I had vague memories of a room with clear walls and a woman with a sharp voice, but trying to think back to it had my head throbbing. It was like staring at my reflection in a warped mirror or a stormy lake.

All I knew was that there was a woman I needed to find. She was in danger. Her scent was all I could smell. It was faint, so much so that I wondered if I was imagining it. Granted, there were dozens of feet of earth between me and her.

Realistically, I shouldn't be able to smell her at all. I could be on a fool's errand, wandering aimlessly after a *fifolet*. I reached a junction and stopped, trying to get my bearings. I closed my eyes and drew in a breath. Her scent was stronger to the right, so I turned that way.

Suddenly, I got a burst of her and stopped walking, turning to look for the source. I almost missed the small air vent carved into the ceiling. I was getting closer.

* * * *

I waited — barely — until I felt the sun set before I made my way up out of the hidden tunnels into what was apparently a city drainage system. It was new, to me at least. I had no memories of anything but catacombs, but clearly I'd been asleep for longer than I'd realized.

Not asleep, a small part of me whispered. *Drugged into bloodlust...*

I cringed. Eventually, I would have to track down those missing memories. How long had I been trapped in it? How much had I missed?

As I climbed up a strangely perfect metal ladder and into the city proper, I knew I'd missed even more than I'd realized. The last I remembered, the city had been rebuilding from two back-to-back disastrous fires. Seventeen ninety-four had been a hard year, thousands of buildings lost to the flames. It had been an interesting time, an architect's wet dream. Wood gave way to stone and wrought iron. Our coven's Sanctuary had been one of the earliest to adapt.

The street I found myself standing in had the skeleton of that city — the buildings the same form and function, the balconies the same fleur-de-lis design. But this was not that city. Strange metal beasts barreled down hard stretches of what looked like black rivers — too soft to be stone but too hard to be water. Even the paving stones I was standing on were wrong...too perfect, too square.

Even the language that surrounded me was unfamiliar. English, but not the English I was used to, French words interspersed in an accent that wasn't familiar. Napoleon had just sold our colony to the Americans in my memories. Had the Americans sold us back?

There were too many questions. Answering them would mean risking losing the scent. Already, I could sense that it was hours old and fading fast.

Keeping as far from the black river road — and its metal monsters — I followed it.

Chapter Fourteen

Andromeda Dianus

I woke on a bed of moss, my arousal finally waning. Not sated — I'd need more than a wet dream, even one as hot as that — to ease the sunlust entirely. My thighs ached, muscles sore like I'd just run a marathon, and I could feel the stickiness coating my skin. If there was anyone else around, I'd be embarrassed.

I should have known better than to try scrying. On the one hand, I now had a direction, at least. 'North' was awfully vague, but the magic was still lingering around me. I trusted it would guide me where I needed to go…eventually. I just hadn't expected that it would ramp up my sunlust at the same time.

Magic could be a real bitch sometimes.

Even more so when it urged me to leave the boardwalk behind and head into the swamp proper. At least the trails were easy to follow, even if the magic seemed so exasperating that I refused to just follow a straight line through. I barely enjoyed swimming in a sterile pool, let alone…*this.*

It was well after nightfall, and I was getting paranoid — though could it really be called 'paranoia' if people were actually after you? — when the magic started singing with excitement. I was close.

A few steps later and I caught the scent of Lycans — a lot of them — fifty, at least, and that was a conservative estimate. I slowed down, my heart racing. I didn't think this through… I was a vampire walking into a Lycan encampment…alone.

There were so many ways this could go wrong and so very few ways it could go right.

Before I could decide how to approach, a snarling wolf leapt out from the shadow of a cypress tree, landing on the path in front of me. I shrieked, stumbling back. Only pure luck kept me from falling on my ass, though it didn't save me from stepping into knee-deep swamp water in my hurry to catch myself.

The Lycan made a snorting sound I suspected was a laugh but didn't shift back to his — definitely *his* — biped form. Instead, he dropped back onto his haunches and howled. The sound was ear-splittingly loud. Immediately, several barking yips sounded in reply.

Moments later, I was surrounded.

"Fuck." The expletive slipped out, and a few wolves growled a warning. Slowly, I lifted my hands in the universal sign of peace. "Please, I'm here to see Alpha Roan Silverthorne. I don't mean any harm…"

The first wolf — he was much larger than the others, I realized, his fur dark and brindled — chuffed out another barking laugh. I felt like I should be offended. I *could* have been a threat if I wanted to be.

A moment later, I felt a surge of magic. I was staring right at the wolf, but I couldn't have described the shift from wolf to man if my life depended on it. "I'm Micah," the Lycan said, crossing his arms over his slender chest. He looked too small to have been such a large wolf. "What do you want with my brother?"

"I need his help."

* * * *

Roan Silverthorne

"Alpha! Alpha!" A guard came skidding into the office.

I plonked my head down on the desk, my skull hitting with a resounding thud. "Ow," I groaned, rubbing my forehead. Probably that wasn't the smartest idea, but really? Was ten minutes too much to ask? I'd just barely gotten back from dropping Zerek off to his worried parents with instructions from the vet.

"Dude, not smart," Jonas joked, just laughing when I lifted my head to glare at him. He had too much dirt on me from our childhood — we'd run in the same circles — for me to bring up any of the 'not smart' things he'd done in the past.

Like when he'd gone skinny dipping in the marsh, or when he tried to ghost a *literal* ghost, who'd gotten so angry she'd haunted him for almost a year.

"Did you need something, or are you just here to get in my hair?"

"As fun as that sounds, no. I'm here for a reason. There's a...uh, visitor? To see you?" Jonas stumbled over his words, and I frowned. He wasn't the type of person to think before he spoke.

"A visitor?" I clarified, wondering who it could be. My first guess would have been more refugees, but that wouldn't have had him stumbling, nor would they have needed *me* for that. By now, we had a pretty well-oiled system going, and we'd already agreed we could take another six wolves — at most — before we'd have to regretfully start turning them away.

Maybe it was another pack leader? There'd been rumors of grumblings from a few of them, mostly the ones who'd lost several families recently to my pack. The exodus made them look bad. I checked in with my wolf, though, and he reassured me none of the wards set up along the edge of our territory had been tripped.

Whoever was visiting, their intentions weren't violent.

"Yeah, but you gotta come see this…" Jonas finally looked something other than worried, though I'm not sure glee was a good sign.

I swiped my hand over my face and sighed. "Can't you just tell me?"

"I'll give you a hint. It's a *woman*." He waggled his eyebrows.

"You look insane," I grumbled but broke down, closing the accounting logs for the brewery. Everything *but* the accounting was handled on site, in offices one floor above the distillery.

"You're just jealous," Jonas said, backing out of the room as I stood up but not breaking eye contact.

"Of your janky eyebrows? Not likely." I followed him out into the hall. Thankfully, most of the wolves preferred to spend as much time as possible outside, so

I only had to dodge a handful of people on our way to the door.

"The ladies love 'em," Jonas said, then grinned, winking back at me. "Though I suppose if you have *ladies* following you back from the city, then you must do all right."

"She's from the city?" I jogged up beside him, barely restraining my grin at his subtle curse when he realized what he'd let slip. "Red hair?" I pressed, wondering if I could have really gotten that lucky.

Interspecies mating had occurred before, but it was rare. Typically, our mates—when they weren't wolves, anyway—still felt the mate call, but nowhere near as strongly as we did.

"I was so hoping to see the look on your face," Jonas groaned but nodded. "It's her, right? Your mate? Jonas said you found her but that she was one of the leeches..."

I nodded. "Unfortunately, since it meant our first meeting was *less* than optimal. I'm honestly kind of surprised her dad doesn't have her locked away in a tower, the way he acted." Unless he *had* tried to lock her away, and that was why she'd come to me. Was she in danger?

My smile faded at the thought, and I sped up. It didn't take much effort to guess her location. I could hear a large group of wolves near the west end, yipping and huffing. As I hurried toward the sound, I tried to pinpoint it. It wasn't excitement, per se...but not aggression, either.

Cautious curiosity, maybe. That was the closest I could get to identifying their mood without seeing them. I rounded the corner of the cabin at the end and froze.

I couldn't say that I didn't want to see the pretty redhead I'd fantasized about earlier on her knees without being a dirty rotten liar. The most I could say honestly was that *these* weren't the circumstances I wanted that sight to be in.

On her knees, surrounded by over a dozen, shifted wolves, all of them standing still and rigid. I scanned them quickly. While most were on alert, at least none were showing outright aggression.

The expression on Princess Andromeda's face, though, caught my attention and held it.

Being surrounded by almost a dozen wolves in the middle of the Bayou, I'd have expected more fear and less annoyance. Honestly, she looked more disgusted at the state of her jeans than anything.

"Well, well. Look what we got here," I called out as I approached the circle, plastering on a wide, friendly smile. "Your daddy send you out here to renegotiate?"

Her skin paled slightly as she looked away from my younger brother to stare at me instead. Then, she set her jaw and shook her head. "I need to talk to you."

"Okay," I drawled, waiting for her to start talking, but she just stared at me. Slowly, her expression shifted. I couldn't help getting the feeling like she was thinking to herself that I was a moron with the way she was staring. "You gonna talk, or…"

"Alone," the vampire princess snapped. I barely resisted the urge to reach down and adjust the erection growing in my jeans. Beside me, my brother chuckled, likely amused by the growing scent of my pheromones. I swatted him over the head. It wasn't my fault that my inner wolf found her demandingness attractive.

I'd always loved a good brat.

"Hell no!" My brother said before I could answer, the sound chorused by the growl of several wolves.

To her credit, she didn't flinch.

"Sorry, Princess, but you'll need to tell me *something* before we'll let you into our humble little village," I said, agreeing with my brother, just a bit more diplomatically.

Her skin flushed with anger, getting pinker than I thought possible for a vampire. It made me wonder what else I could do to get her to flush... I cleared my throat, dragging my mind away from that image.

"Don't call me 'princess'," she snapped, thankfully not seeming to notice the little side trip my thoughts were going on.

"You know, *Princess,*" Micah over-emphasized the title this time, "you're not really in a place to be making demands."

If it wasn't for the fact that he was right, I might have scolded him for his undiplomatic response. But my second *was* right... I really did need some information if I expected my guards to allow her to stay in my presence alone.

Mate or not, she was still a vampire. They didn't have a great track record for trustworthiness.

Andromeda wilted. The collar of her blouse slipped down the curve of her shoulder until she tugged it roughly back up. She stayed quiet for long enough that I considered turning around and going back to my office to continue working on the books. Before I could, she finally sighed, dropping her eyes to the mud. "My father's been attacked. I...I need your help."

Beside me, my brother sucked in a breath to match mine. It had been centuries—longer, even—since a coven leader had been killed. In addition to the leeches being just in general hard to get rid of, the older ones had been rumored to even be able regenerate limbs if needed.

Considering how difficult they were to kill, few people even bothered to try. "None of my people would have done this," I said, crossing my arms as I stared her down.

"I know," she immediately replied, meeting my gaze firmly, "though I wouldn't be surprised to hear rumors of it. I know who did it, or…well, at least who's behind it.

"So what do you need from me? If you don't think it was one of us?"

Her gaze skirted across the circle of wolves before returning to mine. "I…I don't know who to trust. She — Arlow, my father's mistress," Princess Andromeda clarified, "wouldn't have been working alone. It's not her style. If I ask the other covens for help, they're just as likely to strike at us while we're weakened as provide aid, but I don't know who of my coven has been compromised."

I exchanged glances with my brother before slowly nodding. She was right. The situation was too delicate to risk trusting anyone. My chest warmed as I realized that she'd come here. Some part of her, however small, had trusted me.

"I'll help how I can," I finally said, stepping forward and stretching out my hand.

She hesitated only a second before she placed her palm in mine. It was small and delicate, but her grip was strong. I helped her stand, allowing our hands to linger together for another second. Reluctantly, I released her.

"Welcome, Princess Andromeda, to the Silverthorne pack."

Chapter Fifteen

Andromeda Dianus

I followed the Alpha and his...beta? — the younger wolf looked so much like the Alpha that I assumed they were siblings — through the center of the village toward what they apparently called the packhouse. Except for being slightly longer and two stories instead of one, it looked nearly identical to the ones we'd just passed.

Compared to our Sanctuary, these looked humble — clearly built by hand out of cut timber, with only a few simple, single-paned windows spaced unevenly across and a broken pitch roof. The smaller cabins almost seemed to hover above the ground, raised as they were on cinder blocks. The supports of the packhouse, on the other hand, were larger and spaced closer together to support the weight.

Still, I shivered at the idea of weathering a hurricane in one of them. As a vampire, I couldn't drown, but that didn't mean I *enjoyed* the thought of sitting in a house as it floated away along a river.

The packhouse interior was warmer than I expected and not just temperature-wise. It was obvious that the Lycans had decorated it with care. Paintings, clearly done by amateurs who loved art rather than true artists, hung from twine draped over nails on each wall, interspersed with beaded murals.

The large open room we walked into was crowded, too many tables taking up most of the space to the left, handmade chairs pushed as close to one another as they could get. The right half of the room had been turned into a makeshift shelter of sorts. Blankets were piled haphazardly every few feet, boxes of belongings separating one sleeping area from the next.

"What is this place?" I asked as we reached the end of the room, looking over my shoulder at it as we passed into a hallway.

"The packhouse? Normally, it's where we hold meetings, community dinners, things like that," Alpha Roan explained, leading me to a plain door on the left-hand side of the hallway and holding it open. I tried not to show my nerves as I preceded him inside, into what was apparently a study.

Though even in here, a nest of blankets rested on top of the hand-woven red rug.

Alpha Roan followed me in, circling around the desk to drop into the chair. For once, it wasn't handmade. It was one of the wheeled, plastic ones from the office supply stores. They had dozens of them just like that back at the Sanctuary for the clerks to use.

"Micah," Roan said as the younger wolf started to follow him inside. "Please go check on the pups. Make sure no more are messing with the crawfish."

"You can't *really* think I'd leave you *alone* – " The younger wolf started to argue but a stern look from the Alpha silenced him. He didn't look happy about it, but finally, he nodded. "Yes, Alpha," he grumbled as he left, shutting the door hard behind him.

"Am I interrupting one, then? A meeting, I mean?" I asked as I carefully perched in the chair opposite him.

"Not at all," Alpha Roan said, and his smile actually looked genuine. "I was just working on some paperwork before you got here, but nothing that can't wait until later."

"Oh, I just meant… I mean, it looked like people were sleeping on the floor, that's all," I clarified, trying not to sound rude but genuinely curious.

Understanding filled his eyes. "Ah, *that*. Our pack is growing rapidly. We're building housing as quickly as we can" – which explained the several half-started cabins we'd walked past on our way – "but for every cabin we finish, two more families arrive."

I shifted in my seat. The Lycans were better organized than I'd expected – my dad had always said they were little better than animals, but clearly, he'd been wrong – and I found myself feeling guilty for the luxurious mansion I'd lived in my whole life, knowing that there were families here sleeping on the floor.

"Anyway," Roan said, changing the subject, "you didn't come here to hear about that. We don't have much, but what we do have, we're willing to share."

"I appreciate your help. I'll try to stay out from underfoot, and I promise I don't need much. I can help reinforce your wards while I'm here, if you'd like?" I'd given most of my money to the cabbie to get here, but that didn't mean I couldn't pay my way in trade.

"We'd appreciate it. Might be a good idea if you're staying a while anyway. This Arlow lady, does she know you're here?" Roan's smile gave way to seriousness.

I shook my head. "No...or at least I don't think so. I didn't even know I was coming until I'd already left the Sanctuary. I'm hoping she'll look for me at one of the other covens, or the safehouses." I picked at the drying mud on my jeans. For now, I was safe here, but...for how long?

How long until she gave up chasing rumors and hired a witch to scry for me?

Dark images rose unbidden in my mind. Visions of her tracking me here and slaughtering the whole pack of Lycans to get to me—or of my father waking from his healing sleep only to rise from the dirt right into her clutches.

I closed my eyes in pain. Neither of those options was acceptable, which left...

"I need to call the Collective," I realized, opening my eyes just in time to see him fumble the pen he was just picking up, dropping it to the desk.

"Shit," he cursed, his skin going pale. "There's no other way?"

Nobody wanted to be the one to draw their eye to them. The Collective was the closest thing to a governing body the supernatural creatures had, mostly because the *fae* were so powerful that only a moron would try to oppose them.

They generally kept their noses out of the day-to-day stuff, but an attempted assassination would get their attention, especially when it happened in a coven as old as ours. And while I might not be able to track down who was working with Arlow — or prove that she was involved — the *fae* could.

Beyond the fact that they couldn't — not wouldn't or didn't, but *couldn't* tell a lie — no one could lie to them, either. I'd only met one twice, back in my youth, and it was two times more than I would have liked.

"I don't know how else to prove that I'm innocent," I reluctantly replied, grimacing at the despair on his face. "If...if you've changed your mind about helping—"

"No," he interrupted, then sank back in his chair with a sigh. "I said I would help, and I will. Call them. They will be"—his face twisted—"welcome on our lands."

"I wasn't able to bring anything with me," I admitted, gesturing down at myself. "Just what I had on at the time. Well, not even that because I'd still had to buy the boots. I don't suppose you have a set of windchimes? And maybe some honey?" It would be the simplest circle I've ever laid, but unlike demons, the *fae* weren't tied as strictly to rituals. It was the *intent* that mattered.

Unfortunately, Alpha Roan shook his head. "The honey I can do, but we only have one set of windchimes and it's iron." He paused, looking thoughtful. "Probably should bury those before they get here, now that I'm thinking of it."

I grimaced. Without windchimes, my options were limited. "Crystals?" I asked, not surprised when he shook his head.

"We can take a trip to town in the morning. I'd rather not take the pirogue on the bayou at night," Alpha Roan said. To his credit, he looked genuinely apologetic. It was that, more than anything, that had me trusting he was legit.

After all, there was still *one* other way to summon the *fae*, and it required just four river rocks, an inch of still water, and two people willing to get naked.

So all I needed...

Was one other person willing to get naked.

I gave Alpha Roan a bright smile.

Chapter Sixteen

Roan Silverthorne

"You can't be serious." Surely, I'd misheard. *Surely,* she hadn't just *casually* suggested we go out into the bayou and fuck like bunnies.

"I can't go back to New Orleans until the situation is handled, and even if someone else is willing to go for me, if my scent is on them, they could be in danger. I don't know how many people might be looking for me by now." She grimaced, then added, "Besides, I don't have any money. I'm not going to expect your pack" — her eyes darted to the blanket on the floor that I've been sleeping on—"to cover the cost. You're easy enough on the eyes." She gave me a once-over so thorough it made me feel like I was standing in front of her naked, "and you already called me your mate, so I doubt you'll have performance anxiety."

She said it all so matter of fact-like that I found myself questioning, again, whether I was hearing what

I thought I was hearing. "So," I clarified, "you have absolutely no problem having ritual sex in the woods and broadcasting it to the entire *fae* realm, just to avoid buying some crystals?"

"It's just sex" — she rolled her eyes — "not a marriage proposal. Though I'm not saying I would say no to a date later, after we get this whole thing settled and my dad is safe."

"About that..." I leaned forward a bit, my earlier curiosity stirring. "What actually happened?"

She winced, rubbing her hand over her neck in what I suspected was meant for comfort. "He was in the middle of what I think was supposed to be a lecture, and he started getting...maudlin? It was odd, anyway. Then he collapsed. Definitely poison, though I could only narrow it down by symptoms to juniper, mayflower or holly." She paused for a second before adding, "Or a combination of them, maybe? Either way, I figured it out quick enough to give him a pseudo-antidote to at least keep him from getting sicker, but without more information, I couldn't guarantee that giving him anything else wouldn't cause a worse reaction. I sent him to the earth, so I have a few weeks, a month at best, to prove my innocence and get all Arlow's minions out of the Sanctuary before he wakes."

Instinctively, I stretched across the desk and took her hand, squeezing it in an attempt to offer comfort. "I'm sorry. That must have been frightening."

Rather than look sad, though, Andromeda chuckled. "Sweet talker, aren't you? Don't worry. You've already got a free ticket into my pants."

"That's not— I d-didn't..." I stammered, releasing her hand like it was on fire.

A smirk stretched across her face and something about the expression made my dick harder than ever in my jeans. I flushed. "Oh, you're too easy, I'm just *teasing*. You know, if you expect us to be mates, you're going to have to get used to my sense of humor."

"Mates... Yes, I um...suppose you're right," I agreed, feeling more off kilter than I think I'd ever felt in my whole life.

Her grin softened. "Would you prefer a trial run before we do the *faerie* circle? You look a bit nervous."

Her insinuation was the spur I needed to pull myself together. I'd never been concerned about fucking anyone before, and I didn't intend on letting nerves get the best of me now. If she wasn't my mate — if my wolf wasn't pacing in my chest, urging me not to screw it up — I wouldn't have been giving it a second thought.

"Don't worry, Princess. I can handle you. But if *you* want to practice first, I won't say no." I winked and leaned back in my chair again, adjusting my dick. The front of my jeans stretched obscenely across it, every considerable inch on display.

And when her eyes dropped right down to it, her pink tongue slipping out to wet her lips, I felt strangely reassured. Part of me had been concerned that she was only suggesting sex to save her father, which left me feeling gross. Knowing that she wanted this...wanted *me*...made it easier to consider it seriously.

I didn't have to say anything else. She stood before I could. She hooked her thumbs in the waistband of her jeans but otherwise, made no move to strip. Instead, she strutted around the desk, slipping into the narrow space between it and my knees. Her movements were graceful as she, without removing her hands from her jeans, slid onto the desk and slowly spread her thighs.

My wolf clawed himself closer to the surface, and I clenched my hands on the arms of my chair as I struggled to keep him from taking over. "Tell me what you want, Princess, because once we get started, I'm not going to want to stop," I promised.

Her skin flushed, lilac darkening her cheeks. "Who says I'm going to want you to?"

I felt wild and feral as I slowly stood, stepping even closer. As a vampire, she had no body heat to share, but in this summer warmth, the chill from her skin felt even better than if she did.

"Andromeda—" I started to warn her, but she interrupted me.

"Andy. Please, call me Andy."

"Andy," I corrected, her name coming out of my throat like a purr, "this isn't going to be soft, and I don't *do* gentle." On the last word, I moved quick. With her vamp speed, I knew she'd be able to avoid my hand if she wished—but she didn't. I closed my hand around her throat and squeezed, not hard enough to cut off her air completely but enough that she froze. Her eyes darkened from honey to chocolate, parting her lips on a gasp.

"So," I murmured, leaning in until my breath skimmed over the line of her jaw, "if that doesn't sound like something you're into, tell me now." I loosened my hand just enough for her to speak if she wished.

She stayed silent but her breathing sped up.

"Going once, going twice..."

Silence was my only answer. My grin grew more feral as my wolf crept closer to the surface. I knew if I looked in a mirror, my eyes would be burning gold. "Mine now," he growled from my throat, the sound deep and possessive. I felt her shiver. My hand flexed on her skin, her pulse thudding against my palm. Fast, it fluttered, like the wings of a hummingbird, but powerful.

"Undo your jeans," I ordered, watching her eyes. She was no waif-thin, blonde-haired, blue-eyed beauty. It was that very fact that made me stare. Every time I looked at her, I saw something new, unique to her. From the scattering of violet freckles across the narrow bridge of her nose to the beauty mark resting in the hollow of her throat—and her eyes, globes of liquid brown that should have looked average but were flecked with gold leaf.

I kept her gaze until I heard the button pop open, then looked down, watching her nimble fingers work her zipper lower. It opened to more flesh, an expanse of pale skin exposed slowly.

"Good girl," I murmured, leaning in to trace my lips over the shell of her ear. At the same time, I used my free arm to sweep the desk clear. Pens and pads of papers, boxes of staples and paperclips all went flying. I heard them land and skitter away, likely rolling under the desk and into shadows where I'd only find them later with the vacuum, but I didn't care.

With my other hand, the one still wrapped around her throat, I urged her onto her back. Her copper-flame hair fanned across the surface of the desk, several locks trailing over the edge, a mirror to her legs.

In a quick move, I released her for a second, but only to grab her by the thighs and scoot her backward, until her ass hovered just above the edge. "Hands over your head, Kitten." My leer grew stronger as she obeyed. The move pulled up the hem of her shirt, exposing an expanse of silken flesh.

I couldn't resist.

I caved to my wolf's demand and leaned over her, nipping at her belly in a show of dominance. It flexed beneath my mouth, caving in as she drew in a sharp breath and quivering when I swirled my tongue into her belly button. I moaned at the taste of her skin, my excitement growing. If her belly tasted so good, how did she taste lower?

I couldn't wait any longer to find out.

I yanked on the fabric of her jeans, stepping back for only as long as it took to work the mud-sticky fabric down her legs, pausing to unzip her boots and tug them off. Her socks came free with the pants. Then, I stepped closer again, into the cradle of her hips. I ran my palms up her thighs, digging my thumbs into the taut tendons surrounding the perfect folds of her, her sex bare to my eyes.

"No panties, naughty girl? Tell me, did you take them off before you came to ask for my aid, or were you like this in the throne room?" I teased, stroking every inch of exposed skin except where I knew she wanted to be touched. "If I'd pinned you to that wall then shoved my hand in your jeans, would I have found you wet for me, ready for plundering?"

"Yes!" she yelped. Her thighs clamped on my hips as she used the leverage to lift hers, a nonverbal plea for touch.

"Yes, what, Kitten? Yes, you took them off just for me? If I'd refused to aid you, was this your back-up plan?" I gripped her thighs and forced them apart until her hips fell back to the desk. Then, I pushed them up, far enough that the lips of her sex gaped open to reveal the impossibly tiny hole they were hiding. She was dripping slick. It clung to her lower lips like morning dew.

"No, not...not my back-up plan. Just...just my hope," she panted, and when I glanced up, I saw her knuckles whiten against the desk's edge like she was clinging on with every bit of strength she had. Divots were forming in the wood, but I didn't care.

She could break my desk as many times as she wanted as long as I got to break *her* first.

"Pretty little slut," I murmured, watching her face as I said it. Not all women liked that, and while I told her I didn't fuck gentle, I also didn't fuck *mean*. But her mouth just opened on a moan, her eyes fluttering closed for a second as her back bowed. "Oh, you like that?" I continued, tightening my hands on the back of her thighs. "Want to be my dirty little whore?"

"Yes, *please!*" Her curls bobbed as she tossed her head, the cords of her neck in sharp relief beneath her skin. My teeth ached to bite it, but I wouldn't do that, not without careful discussion first, not without knowing that she knew what it meant.

I let go of one of her thighs. As if by instinct, she started to lower it, but I swatted her inner thigh with my hand. "Keep it there," I ordered, waiting until she put it back where I wanted it before I moved, stripping off her shirt and tossing it aside. "Good girl," I praised.

Her breasts were small, not quite as large as my hand when I cupped one, but they were firm and the nipples pert, digging into my palm like little diamonds. I gave it a gentle squeeze before I released it—only to take the erect nipple between my thumb and forefinger and pinch.

She yelped, so I did the same to her other breast. The way her skin flushed, though—the lilac heat spreading from her cheeks all the way down her neck to her chest — she liked it. I pinched harder and said, "Tell me when to stop."

"Don't!" she blurted, then I watched her pearlescent teeth dig into the soft flesh of her lower lip.

"Don't be embarrassed about what you like, Kitten," I said with a grin, giving her nipple a little twist. "I'm not against a little pain play."

Her gaze met mine, curiosity easy to read. "Most people think it's odd, or...or a call for help," she explained. "I don't want broken bones, but...bruises could be fun."

"I can do bruises," I promised, leaning down again to suck one onto the curve of her left breast, just above the nipple I was still manipulating in my fingers. I let go of her other thigh, trusting her to keep it where I wanted, so I could pinch her other nipple as well. I loved how it felt, the initial softness of the cool, lavender skin before I felt the harder bead at its center. I rolled them in my hands until she was a moaning mess, her hips pushing up to meet mine.

I released her flesh from my mouth to say, "I didn't say you could move, did I?"

"No, Alpha..." she cried, and though I hadn't thought my dick could get any harder, hearing my title on her lips like a curse turned me to steel, the zipper of my jeans painful against it.

"Consider yourself lucky I'm in a giving mood," I purred, then straightened up to standing. I kept a smile on, but inwardly, I hated losing contact with her skin, her flesh, the pleasant softness of her curves. Instead, I sat back in my chair, grateful that my bulk had made an armless one more practical.

I slouched, knees spreading as I put my erection on full display. "Climb on, Kitten."

She leaned up on her elbows, eyes wide. "What?"

I patted my erection over the zipper. "I want you to get yourself off on my jeans. Unless you'd rather hump my leg like a bitch?" I lifted my eyebrow as I stretched out one denim-covered leg. Like most wolves, I was barefoot, shoes a thing we reserved for trips into town — and only then because the humans required it.

She slid slowly, almost uncertainly, off the desk, but there was a fire in her gaze that told me she was into it, that she *wanted* this. Then she climbed, graceful as a panther, into my lap.

She shifted around, unable to settle, and it took me a second longer than it should have to realize she was doing it on purpose — that each shift of her lower lips across my covered dick was a tease.

I gripped her hips and held her still, thrusting up to meet her sex with mine as I groaned. "Brat," I scolded, panting out a breath as I held her steady long enough to get myself under control.

She quirked her lips upward, until I caught the lower one between my teeth. I bit down, releasing it just shy of breaking the skin, then ran my tongue across it. When I pulled back, her lip was swollen and glistening.

Slowly, I released my tight grip on her hips, sliding my palms down the outside of her thighs instead. "Now, Kitten. I want to feel you come like this."

Her muscles bunched under my hands as she started to rock, each motion rubbing her soaked pussy against my dick. Within seconds, I could feel her slick soaking through my jeans, and it took everything I had to sit still.

I heard her breath catch after a particularly hard grind, knowing she'd caught her clit on the rough denim. "There you go," I murmured, finally giving in.

I leaned forward and took her nipple between my lips. It felt even colder in the heat of my mouth as I started to suck. She moaned, loud enough the whole pack likely knew what we were up to. I didn't care.

Wolves weren't prudish by nature. I'd seen many a couple copulating in the main hall.

A nip of my teeth had her back arching, like she was trying to smother me with her breast, and the sexy thought tore a growl from my throat. The sound only seemed to make her hotter. I could smell her gushing slickness, feel her quivering beneath my hands.

"Close," she whimpered, her hips stuttering with the strain of her movements.

Nice person that I was, I decided to help her. I slid my hands up her thighs again and took her hips in a tight grip, pulling her down until she yelped, the button of my jeans clearly hitting her clit just right.

Then, I kept her there, thrusting up against it until she screamed, her whole body shuddering. By now, my jeans were soaked, and I felt like I was torturing myself with waiting. I knew it would be worth it. There was nothing I found hotter than burying myself into a dripping wet cunt.

I waited until her climax faded before I moved, carrying her with me as I stood. I didn't lay her back on the desk. Instead, I carried her around it to the nest of blankets and pillows on the floor. She gripped my shoulders tight as I lowered her carefully.

If I had a bed, I'd have thrown her on it. I would have loved to see her breasts jiggle as she landed, hear the soft exclamation of breath. It wasn't meant to be, not this time.

I opened my jeans and grinned. "There. Now that we've got the edge off…"

Chapter Seventeen

Andromeda Dianus

Roan's smile was sharp as a devil's as he loomed over me, opening his jeans to pull out the monster between his legs. I'd been with many men throughout my life, some of whom I was sure had been bigger, but I couldn't think of any now in the moment.

His cock was as thick as my wrist at the base, his helmet even larger and flushed nearly purple. Pre-cum dripped from his slit, tracing the line of a prominent vein down the side. My mouth watered at the sight.

"On your knees, Kitten," he ordered, and I scrambled to obey. Even with the nest of blankets, I could feel the wood floor hard beneath them, but I didn't care. I peered up at him through my lashes, hoping he was going to let me taste him.

Then, I realized I didn't have to rely on hope. "Please, Alpha, can I taste you?" I asked, licking my lips in a way I knew would bring his attention to them. I was right. His eyes were glowing as he stared at me, and I knew it wasn't my imagination that his fist tightened around his dick like a cock ring.

"Oh, you're going to taste me all right. I'm going to fuck your throat until I'm *all* you taste," he growled, and there was nothing in the world like that sound. The danger behind it, the pure, animalistic wildness... If I hadn't *just* come, I might have just from hearing it. "Open your mouth."

I did, stretching my jaw as wide as I could. Even still, he barely fit. The thick head of his dick pressed against my tongue as he slid in, coating it in his salty pre-cum. A little treat before the main course, I thought, before I wasn't able to think about anything anymore.

He didn't take it easy on me, curling one strong hand around the back of my skull, holding me in place, while the other wrapped around my throat. He moved slowly, but there was a surety to each pump of his hips, a knowledge that he was moving with both care and purpose and that there was nothing I could do to stop him.

Then it happened... On one particularly brutal thrust in, the tip of his dick slid into my throat and I choked, instinctively trying to pull away. All I succeeded in doing was scraping his dick with my teeth, the extra-sharp canine leaving the taste of honey and moonlight on my tongue.

Blood...

I froze, eyes I didn't realize I'd shut snapping open in horror as I met his, but he didn't look angry. Well, he *did*, his face twisted in a pain-pleasure expression, but it was a raw thing — an *I'm-on-the-edge-of-coming* thing I recognized without him even needing to speak.

Then he was moving again, a bit slower, but each time he entered my mouth, I tasted his blood mixing with the pre-cum and I'd never tasted anything sweeter. I moaned, feeling the dampness pooling on my sex again, an itch I couldn't scratch.

My hand moved, seemingly of its own accord, toward my pussy, but Roan moved quickly. He lifted his bare foot, kicking my hand away and stepping on it, pinning it to the blankets with enough strength to keep it there but not enough to hurt. The sole of his foot was as hot as a brand on my skin.

"*Mine*," he growled. "And you won't touch it until I say you can."

Fuck. My curse got tangled in my throat, little more than a vibration against his dick, and it must have felt good, because Roan cursed out loud, tightening his hands against me. He pulled out of my throat, and I whined at the lost, trying to chase the taste, but he held me in place.

"Such a hot mouth, Kitten," he praised. "But if you keep that up, we'll be done too soon. You're a talented little cocksucker."

It should have been insulting, a degradation, but instead, the words were a caress against my skin, a compliment I wanted to roll around in for ages. It had goosebumps lifting on my skin, despite the summer heat.

"I want you on your stomach, ass in the air," the Alpha ordered as he released me, and I scrambled to obey.

If the coven could see you now, a small inner voice said, but I smothered it. I didn't ask to be the heir, didn't want it...all I wanted was *this,* in this moment—to be free to live my life as I chose, to be as much or as little as I wanted.

Right now, I wanted to be his cocksucker, his perfect little whore, his kitten. Just...*his.*

Is this what it means to be mates? This instinctive need to please and submit? Or has it been inside me all along, buried under the weight of status and expectation? Has he made me this...or is this who I've always been?

I found myself wondering, but then I realized that the answers didn't matter. I didn't care if I was learning new things about myself now, nor did I care if it was some...some side-effect from his pheromones or lingering effects from the sun.

If he didn't put his dick in me soon, I was going to burn from the inside out.

"Please, Alpha, take me," I cried out as I obediently lifted my ass, feeling the air against my pussy. Without needing to look, I knew he was staring. I could *feel* his gaze on my core, the heat of it. Then, I heard the sound of him stripping, his jeans landing on the ground and him kicking them aside.

Without warning, he sank his teeth into the soft flesh of my ass. It was never as toned as I wanted it, no matter how many squats I did or herbs I took, but he didn't seem to mind. In fact, he seemed to enjoy it, laying a trail of bite marks across first my left cheek, then my right, until he spread them apart and his hot mouth landed right on my slit. His tongue — God, how could any tongue be that long? — slid from my clit all the way up to my puckered rosebud in a smooth sweep.

I pressed my chest harder to the ground in an attempt to lift my ass even higher, to get his mouth back to where I wanted it.

Instead, he just chuckled, his breath teasing my folds but not touching as he sat back, leaving me empty.

Not for long, though. Without warning, he plunged two fingers into my pussy, curving them in an expert move until he found my G-spot. He rubbed it relentlessly until I was a gibbering, quivering mess, my fingers tangled in the blankets as I sobbed.

He brought me off again. "Look what you did," he scolded as he removed his fingers, shoving them in front of my face. They were coated in slick, and it pooled into the dip of his palm. "Messy girl," he said, but *fuck*, he sounded so goddamn proud. My limbs felt weak, like jelly as I struggled to keep my ass up when all I wanted to do was melt into a puddle.

But I wanted his dick more than that. "Please, Alpha...I need —"

"I know what you need," he said, then he pulled his hand back. I moaned when I heard the dirty sound of him slicking his dick with *my* slick. I wasn't a virgin, so I knew what it sounded like. I'd never gotten so hot by it before, though. The thought of a man jacking off when my holes — any one of them, I wasn't picky — were available had always seemed insulting.

Now, though... God, the thought that he was going to make me wait, that he was stroking himself off, using me like visual porn... Why was that so hot?

I moaned, my back arching, and he swatted my ass in punishment. "Stay still, Kitten. Let me look at you."

It was hard not to move, but I realized he would stop if I did, and as hot as a spanking sounded, it wasn't what I wanted right now. My pussy ached, empty and begging to be filled. I was desperate to at least squeeze my thighs together, knowing the pressure would give me some relief, but I didn't.

Finally, *finally*, I felt the heat of his cock against my entrance. "Don't worry, Andy. I know what you need," he said as he pushed forward, burying his large, thick cock in my cunt in a single smooth motion until his balls rested against my skin and I felt like I was impaled, stretched to the limit.

Except he didn't agree, and clearly, he was right, because a moment later, his finger, still wet with the evidence of my arousal, brushed against my ass. I clenched in surprise then moaned as I felt my sheathe tighten on Roan's dick.

"I'll stop if you tell me to," Alpha said — *warned*? Was it a promise or a threat? My mind was too fuzzy to work through it, then he was slipping his finger, slow but steady, into the tight channel of my ass. It was nowhere near as thick or as long as his dick, but by no means did that mean his fingers were in any way *small*.

It burned, but it was the best kind of pain. "Move, please move, Alpha. I'm *dying*," I begged, barely aware of the words spilling from my lips.

He just laughed, but then he was moving. He was so fucking big that each thrust in felt like he was fisting me — *fuck, what would it feel like if he was fisting me?* — and each slow drag out felt like he was taking my insides with him.

"Oh fuck," I cried out after a particularly hard thrust, and he slid a second finger into my ass and that was it. I was coming again, my pussy spasming as I clenched around him, and that, apparently, was all it took to send him over.

I felt the heat of his seed flooding me with each pulse. He pulled his fingers from my ass and gripped my hips tight. I'd have bruises later in the shape of his fingers, but I didn't care. He grunted, the animalistic sound sending a few last, futile spasms to my cunt.

Then, I collapsed on my belly, my breathing ragged, too worn out to move. And he fell forward as well, his sweaty chest plastered to my back, and his breath was rough as well. But his lips were soft as he pressed them to the back of my neck, nipping in what felt like a playful love bite.

It was perfect…until someone started clapping and I tensed. Roan's body turned to steel against me then he was moving, grabbing a blanket and dragging it over me to hide my nudity.

It seemed Alpha Roan hadn't gotten quite that far yet. He was growling, the sound coming deep from his chest, and he looked like he was two seconds away from trying to tear the man apart.

I grabbed Roan's arm and yanked him back down, hissing, "*He's a fae!*"

"Oooh, it normally takes them so much longer." The twink's grin widened as he shook his head, looking unreasonably proud. "She's a smart one. You should keep her," he said to Roan like he was telling a secret.

"What…? How did you get here?" I asked before Roan could say something that would end with our murdered, dismembered bodies. "We didn't do the ritual…"

"You had what I will admit was a *hot*"—he fanned himself as he said it—"bout of lovemaking right after thinking about us an *obscene* number of times. What more of an invitation did we need to come watch, hm?" He lifted a perfectly sculpted brow.

"I…I thought we needed the river stones? An invitation?" I blurted, wondering at the same time how many *other* times I'd had sex and the fae had just...used it as their personal porn subscription.

"Have you not looked outside? There are stones *everywhere*. It would be nearly impossible to *not* have a stone in each of the cardinal directions *somewhere* around you," the fae boy said, rolling his eyes like he thought me an idiot. "And why would we need an invitation? Are you implying that one of us *wouldn't* be welcome at some point?" His voice sharpened as he said the last, his eyes narrowing as they fixed on me.

I shook my head quickly. "No, of course not. I just thought—"

"Well, maybe you should stop that." The fae sniffed imperiously. "Now, the sex is over and you're both starting to smell. Why don't you tell me why you wanted the Collective's attention so I can be on my way to watch the next merry couple, hm?"

My mind went blank, frozen at the realization that if I spoke wrong, they might not take me seriously. Worse, they might side with Arlow, then where would I be? I clutched the blanket tighter to my chest, panic blocking off my ability to talk.

Roan, thankfully, didn't have the same problem. He cleared his throat, and it was the pack Alpha, not my mate, who replied, "The Dianus Coven is under attack."

"Now, that's not exactly true, is it." The fae boy smirked at me. "Dianus, of the Dianus Coven, has been poisoned. The coven itself is not being threatened. Why should we care who leads?"

I scowled and finally found my voice. "If you know of the situation, then you *know* Arlow is behind it, don't you? You can't honestly think *she* would be a good leader."

The fae shrugged. "Good leader, bad? It has little effect on us as a whole. Why would a god care who rules over ants?"

A *god*? I'd known the fae were capricious and thought highly of themselves, but this was pushing it, even for them. I stood up, not caring that the blanket fell to a puddle at my feet and left me exposed. They'd already watched me in the throes of passion, what care did I have that he saw my breasts now?

"You would let the wealthiest, most influential coven fall prey to a silly little girl and not step in? You know of the weapons we hold, and you *know* the dangers of exposure. Do you think Arlow, who has proven time and time again that she cares nothing for tradition or rules, will abide by the laws that *you* set?" My voice grew more heated as I spoke, visions of all the ways she could bring our entire society to ruin running through my head.

Fae boy shrugged. "*If* she breaks our laws. So far, she's only broken yours."

"You can't be serious." Roan snarled, moving to stand by my side. "You really don't care?"

"It's not that I don't *care*. It's certainly unfortunate, but the Collective can't get involved in every petty little squabble your kind gets into." Fae boy fluttered his hand at me rather rudely as he said 'your kind', and I growled in anger.

"Seriously? Seriously! Y'all stuck your nose in when my dad tried changing our coven logo from a diamond to an oval because you didn't like the 'aesthetic' of it!" I was basically screaming by now, my rage reaching a boiling point.

"Well, a diamond was *much* more chic," the boy replied, earnest as could be and looking confused about why I was bringing it up.

I saw my opening and took it, smirking. "You know, *I* heard that Arlow thinks diamonds are *so* last year. If you let her stay in charge, how long until she has our Sanctuary done up in chiffon and our logo some abstract graphic designer's wet dream?"

Immediately, the fae boy's face went pale. "Well...I mean... Surely..." His body shuddered. "No, no, you're right. That woman's taste is...questionable. I... Yes, I think I can convince my father to let me send a delegation... Give me two of your weeks..." He muttered something else, then popped out of the room as if he'd never been there.

I blinked at the empty desk before turning to Roan. His face was the same picture of confusion that I felt. "Did he really just agree to help because he's worried about Arlow's fashion sense?" I asked, nonplussed.

He nodded, meeting my eyes. A few seconds later, we both burst into laughter. It was born more of relief than of true amusement, but the sound had broken the tension.

Chapter Eighteen

Arlow Dianus

"What do you mean, I'm not *allowed* to take over the coven? Not *allowed?* I'm married to the king, you...you...you *imbecile!* Who *else* would get the crown?" This was absolutely ridiculous. There was no way I was letting the stupid little fae boy with his flower-petal dress and bare feet tell *me* what I could or could not do.

"I imagine the king will, once he wakens from the earth," the brat answered, his voice stupidly high, almost squeaky.

"*Wakens from the earth?*" I screeched. "He's dead! I saw that spawn of his bury him in the yard!"

The new head of the King's Guard, who'd taken over after the previous one—a man I'd spent years swaying to my side through sexual favors—had foolishly allowed himself to be murdered by my husband's *other* heir, the crazy one, leaned over and muttered, "Majesty." Oh, how I loved the sound of that. My first order had been for everyone to adopt that as my title, "Your husband still lives. He just went to the dirt for healing."

I hated the way he said it, the condescending tone of voice that made it clear he was calling me stupid, at least in his head. I struck him, my ruby fingernails leaving scratches across his cheek. "I didn't give permission for you to speak," I snapped as an explanation, since I couldn't really say that the punishment was for annoying me.

His face darkened, the anger easy to read, but he leaned back and gave a sharp nod of his head. He was — unfortunately — smart enough not to apologize, so I couldn't justify a second smack.

"Well, *if* he wakes, then he can have his throne back." I'd just have to make sure next time that I did a better job of poisoning him.

Or just stake him through the heart like I should have the first time.

The fae brat danced closer, his bare feet landing on the stone with the sound of bells. "We simply can't allow it. I'm sure you understand. I think…" He looked around the room with narrowed eyes, until his gaze landed on one of the guards. "Him! Yes, he'll be a good regent until the king wakes." The fae skipped over to the guard.

I slammed my hand down in anger on the stupid, ugly armchair that was currently serving as a throne. "No! I'm not letting some common-blooded *peon* take my husband's throne from me!"

"Hush, dear," the brat giggled, brushing invisible lint of the shocked guard's shoulder epaulet. "The grown-ups are talking."

"No!" I screamed, hitting the throne again. "It's not fair! I have put in too much work for you to screw it up now!"

The fae sighed, looking apologetically up at the larger vampire. "Don't worry. You'll be the perfect fit for this until the king wakens. Clearly, you have *much* better taste then *she* does." He waved his hand toward me, and I felt beyond insulted.

"Better taste? Better *taste*? You're trying to strip me of my rightful place in history because he has better *taste*?" I stood up and stomped down the steps of the dais until I could get right in the stupid man's face. "Are you *insane*?"

He narrowed his eyes and something about it sent a chill down my spine. I almost stepped back. "No, but clearly *you* are. Do not forget that with a snap of my fingers, I could turn you back into the dust you were made from." The words were icy cold and sharp, and this time, I shivered. The power leaking from him. I'd never felt anything like it...

"Go," the fae ordered, and I stepped back, toward the throne room doors. "Now, before I *lose* my temper..."

I spun on my heel and fled.

They'd pay for this, all of them...starting with my husband's little bitch of a daughter.

Even without the crown, I had allies who would rally behind me. As soon as I found her, she was *dead*.

Chapter Nineteen

Roan Silverthorne

"You...you expect me to go *outside*?" Andy asked, staring at the window with an expression that looked like shock before she turned back to me.

"Uh-huh," I answered, lifting a brow. I wasn't sure where the confusion was coming from. I thought the answer had been pretty obvious.

"Outside," she clarified again. "Like...out there?" She pointed toward the woods through the window. The expression on her face had me smirking, even if I was still a bit confused, mostly because I wasn't sure where I'd lost her.

"Yeah?" I said slowly, "It's an *outhouse*." Certainly it wasn't something you'd keep in the kitchen?

"And...and I have to go outside?" she repeated herself, her face so bewildered I couldn't help but laugh.

"Yeah...that's why it's called an 'out' house. Because it's 'out' side."

"And you expect me to use it?" she asked, crossing her arms. Thankfully, she'd gotten dressed after our little interlude, because otherwise, I might have gotten distracted.

"I suppose you could use the woods," I answered, dragging my gaze away from her breasts.

"I can't pee in the woods!" she protested, dropping her hands to her hips instead. They were wide, begging for me to grab them again.

Instead, I threw my hands in the air, exasperated with the whole conversation. "Apparently, you can't pee in an outhouse, either!" I turned on my heel and started for my office door, not sure what she wanted but knowing I needed to leave before I bent her over the desk for a second round. I loved seeing her like this, her face indignant about...whatever she was upset about.

"Hey, wait!" she called after me, and when I turned to look at her over my shoulder, she was practically dancing. "I really need to pee..."

"I don't know what to tell you. Pick a tree, pick a bush." I rolled my eyes and jokingly added, "Pick the goddamn rug?" I'd never seen someone get so bent out of shape about peeing before, and it was almost adorable — or would have been, if I didn't feel like I was missing something.

She glanced at the rug and there was something in her face that made me realize she was actually considering it. My chest tightened at the thought of her marking my rug, pissing on it like she was claiming it...

If she did, there was no way I'd be able to stop my wolf from taking over and fucking her against it. "Do it and I'll bring out the newspaper," I barked.

She glared at me, the expression too cute to take seriously. "I'm not a dog!"

"Clearly," I drawled, grinning. "A dog would have pissed twice by now and been done with it!"

"Gah," she screamed, grabbing a fistful of her hair and yanking. I'd have been more than willing to pull her hair, if that was what she wanted. She drew in a breath after a second and smoothed it out. "I mean, don't you have a bathroom? With an indoor toilet, and…and flushing?'

"Yeah…in the outhouse." Really, what on earth was her problem? So she had to step through the backdoor and walk three feet to the trees to get to it. That really didn't seem like a huge deal. It had been easier — and cheaper — to build three separate communal bathrooms throughout the pack than to make sure each individual cabin had a septic tank and indoor plumbing. Besides, the smell was easier to bear this way, tucked into the woods instead of right next to the bedrooms.

Win-win.

She crossed her arms again but must have decided that the walk would be worth it if it meant she got to pee, because she finally waved her hand. "Fine. Take me to" — she visibly cringed — "your outhouse."

"I mean, it's not just mine," I said as I started leading the way. "The pack shares them."

Behind me, I heard her gag, and I rolled my eyes. I knew vampires were kind of stuck up, but this seemed beyond the par. Still, I guess she *was* vampire royalty. I shouldn't have been surprised.

It was after dark, at least, so I knew she wasn't upset because she'd have to go out in the sunlight—though that *was* something I was going to have to consider. Maybe we could get some tarps? Cover the path gap from the back door to the trees so she'd be safe? Though, I'd heard rumors that the Dianus line could go out in sunlight, but I'd rather not risk it if that's all they were.

"It's, um…bigger than I expected," she said when we reached it, before we were able to go inside. I looked at it, trying to see it from her perspective. A twelve-by-twelve cabin with no windows… Not that us wolves were super bothered by privacy—the public sex made it a moot point—but the glass for the windows was expensive, so we'd decided to save them for the cabins.

Besides, none of us had particularly wanted to be in the middle of showering and come face to face with a bear. Some things you just didn't need to see in the bathroom, even if you *were* separated by a centimeter-thick pane of glass. The front door was plain, with a little wooden sign hung from a nail, currently flipped to 'unoccupied'.

I flipped the sign as I opened the door for her and ushered her in. "Here," I said, hurrying after her. "Let me get the lights for you." I hit the switch so she didn't have to, not sure exactly how the whole vampires-make-electricity-fritz thing worked and not willing to risk blowing a bulb—or worse, shorting out the whole system—if we didn't have to.

She stopped abruptly just in front of me. "You call this an outhouse?" She sounded shocked, looking from the porcelain claw-foot tub to the walk-in shower then over to the standard toilet.

"I mean…yes?" Seriously, what was her issue?

"This is like a real bathroom!" she said, turning to glare at me like it was somehow *my* fault.

"I mean, what did you expect, a hole in the ground?" I answered with a laugh and a big smile that faded as I saw her face. "Oh, wait…you did? I mean, just because we like nature doesn't mean we're *animals*." I thought maybe I should be offended by the assumption, but for some reason, I just found it hilarious.

"You kept calling it an outhouse! An outhouse is like…literally a hole in the ground and a bench and maybe a little weird moon in the door!" She got a bit louder, waving her hands around widely in a way that made me want to grab one and suck a fingertip into my mouth. So, I did, grinning around it when she didn't stop me. Instead, she moaned and swayed against my body.

"No, Princess," I said as I released her, smiling down at her indignant expression. "An outhouse is any outbuilding containing a toilet."

"But typically containing no indoor plumbing," she added, clearly still upset. But her lips were turned up in a little smile that made me think that the bathroom itself had actually pleased her.

It was quite nice, if I said so myself. Some of the pack women had taken to decorating, leaving a little wicker baskets full of potpourri on the back of the toilet, candles in glass jars waiting to be lit by the sink. Even the soap, handmade by some of the younger wolves, had been molded into the shape of flowers. They were getting better. The first half-dozen batches had looked more like lumps than roses.

They were talking of selling them at the market in the fall.

"Um…" Andy shifted her weight, looking up at me with pleading eyes. "Can you…? Roan, I *really* have to pee."

"Okay?" I leaned back against the wall and waved to the toilet. "I promise it flushes."

"You're just planning on standing there and watching?" she blurted, her skin turning lavender as she blushed.

"Are you *shy*?" I asked, surprised. "I just had my mouth on your pussy and my fingers in your ass!"

"It's not the same!" she cried out, and I laughed. Her quirkiness was, frankly, adorable.

"Fine. I'll step outside while you *pee*. Can I at least bathe with you, or is that embarrassing, too?"

"That…that would be nice," she mumbled, closing the door behind me as I stepped outside, still chuckling.

"Women are weird," I muttered, shaking my head.

"I heard that!" she hollered, then a moment later, I heard her start to urinate.

"And I heard *that*." I grinned as I called back, opening the door and stepping inside as soon as she flushed. "So stepping outside seems rather pointless."

I hadn't thought her skin could flush any further, but now it was nearly violet. "You're such a dick."

I shoved my pants down and grabbed the dick in question, grinning as I brandished it. "You love it."

Her gaze fixed on it and she licked her lips. "Yeah…yeah, I really do."

"Bath, first," I scolded, though there was nothing I wanted more than to put her on her knees again. But it was an unwritten rule that nobody had sex in the outhouses, since we only had three, and it wasn't fair to make others wait while you did something you could do in the main buildings.

Chapter Twenty

Arsenious Dianus

Even without searching for answers, I found some by accident in my quest to follow her — *her*, the woman from my dreams, the one whose scent beckoned me like a siren's song. Despite the sense of urgency that filled me the longer I searched, I couldn't help gathering information. It had been almost three hundred years since I'd walked these streets — the date stamped on top of a folded paper in a strange metal-and-glass box. And if the title of the paper was right, the city I was in was still called New Orleans. I tried retrieving the paper, but it needed some form of coins to open the box, and I didn't have time to get a job to procure them.

Instead, I headed toward the nearest joining of two black rivers.

Streets, a lady called them, and I'd realized that's what they were. Roads, used much the same as they'd been in my time, just made of strange black rock instead of dirt, and traveled by metal monsters instead of horses.

I learned quickly to wait for the strange candles shaped like people to light up as if by magic before I tried to cross. The metal monsters yelled at me, their voices deep and blaring, if I didn't, and one nearly struck me before I leapt out of the way, my heart pounding in my chest.

I quickly realized how much I missed the tang of adrenaline, but I didn't relish the thought of healing from the injuries I'd likely sustain.

The scent grew stronger outside one building that seemed to sell only shoes — hundreds and hundreds of shoes made from materials I'd never seen before, shoes that smelled like no leather I'd ever encountered — but I didn't go inside, since the scent continued on again.

At the next corner, though, the scent grew faint, smothered in the smoke-and-rubber scent the metal monsters emitted. I growled.

How was I supposed to find her now?

The metal monsters moved too fast for me to try to catch one, their angry bleating sounding every time I tried. I grew frustrated, until one of them finally slowed, moving closer the walking path I was standing on. It stopped between two yellow lines on the black river street.

Then, the side of the monster flung outward like an arm, revealing a human.

Humans...were *inside* the monsters?

Suddenly, my perception of them changed. They weren't metal beasts, moving aimlessly along the streets. They were *carriages*. The humans *drove* them. But where were horses? Had they somehow shrunk them and hidden them inside? Were the horses angry?

Is that what made the growling, grinding noises when they moved?

"Mistress," I blurted, hurrying toward the woman. She yelped, clutching her chest as she looked me over.

"Oh, is this one of those fancy role-playing experiences? I've always wanted to book one," she finally said, lowering her hand as she giggled. I glanced down at my outfit, then at those of the humans bustling along the streets.

I suppose my clothing did look remarkedly different than theirs. My breeches were looser and none of the humans had a waistcoat like mine. Still, the material of my clothing even seemed different then my memories, the stitching neater.

"So? Are you one of those period actors?" The woman's question interrupted my musing over the clothing.

"Uh...yes?" I didn't know what she meant by 'period actor', but if it made her less suspicious of me, I'd go with it. "Mistress, I need assistance. Your carriage... May I use it?"

"My...carriage? Oh, my car?" She looked nervous as she glanced between me and the purple monster. "Um, may I drive you? Uh, be your chauffeur? Is that the right word?"

"Yes!" I didn't know if it was or wasn't, but if she was willing to drive it, then it would save me the time it would take to learn. "How do I get in?"

Chapter Twenty-One

Andromeda Dianus

The water was clear and hot as it filled the tub and smelled faintly of the lavender oil Roan had added before we climbed in. I was grateful the tub was so large. He was a big man on his own, and there were two of us squeezed inside. Despite that, the water had made it to the top of my breasts before he stretched around me, water jostling, to spin the nozzles off. Then, he sank back, pulling me against his chest.

I settled against his warm skin with a sigh. Steam drifted up from the surface of the water, mingling with the smoke from the candles he'd lit. Who knew the wolf was a romantic? I closed my eyes as I snuggled against him. His arm was a warm band under my breasts, keeping me from sliding farther into the bath. I trusted him enough to keep me safe that I allowed myself to relax.

At least until I shifted and felt his dick, mostly soft, under my ass.

A little wiggle had him hardening, and I snuck my hand down between us to take him in hand. "Naughty girl, we shouldn't—" he groaned, breaking off as I gave him an experimental stroke. I quickly discovered he liked a firm grip with a twist at the end. His pre-cum was thicker than the water, letting me feel how much he was leaking, despite the surrounding wetness.

"Shouldn't we?" I purred, not stopping. I twisted slightly, looking up to meet his heated gaze with mine.

"Mm, shouldn't…" he repeated, but he tightened his arm around me and his breath sped up. "Fuck!" He cursed as I ran my thumb across his slit, smearing around the stickiness. "You play dirty, Kitten."

"All's fair," I purred, sitting up and shifting around until I had a thigh on either side of his. They were furry against my skin, something I'd never thought would turn me on this much. "Hands on the side of the tub, Alpha."

He grinned, clearly indulging me, and gripped the porcelain. I waited until he'd done so to line the head of his dick against my cunt. "Hmm," I moaned, rubbing it back and forth, from my clit down to my hole and back.

"Love your dick," I said as I finally sank down on it again. It felt so much bigger like this, reaching into the very center of my core. "So good."

"Ride me, Kitten," he ordered, the depth of his voice making it clear he was still in charge, even if I was the one on top. "Go on. Get yourself off. I want to feel you clenching around me. You're so fucking tight, Princess."

For once, the title didn't hit me like an insult. I sank down on him, again and again, my thighs burning. Every move had his dick stroking me just right inside, and I started fucking him in earnest.

"Your pussy is soaked," he said, but his voice was like a prayer. "God, Kitten, so perfect. Love this cunt. Couldn't have made it better if they sculpted it for my cock... Fuck!" He cursed and let go of the edge of the tub, but I didn't care once he slipped his hand between us. He ran his fingertips over my lower lips, spreading them to better feel himself sliding in and out of my pussy. I grinded against him, and he allowed it for a moment before he removed his hand. Before I could even feel the disappointment, he moved his fingers to my clit instead.

It felt like bolt of lightning hit me, centered on my core, and I cried out as he pinched it. My back arched as if on its own, sending water flooding out of the tub onto the thankfully tiled and angled floor.

He refused to show mercy, rolling and pinching my clit like his personal toy. He gripped my hip with his other hand, holding me in place until my vision started blackening around the edges, and I thought I was going to pass out with the pleasure.

"Come on, Kitten. Come for me," he kept saying, teasing my clit like a fucking sadist. I couldn't take it anymore. *I can't...* Without thinking, I leaned forward, sinking my fangs into his shoulder as I screamed. The taste of him, that sweaty, moonlight copper, was enough to push me over. My pussy clamped around his dick in a stranglehold as I broke down in moans.

"Fuck!" he hollered as he followed me into his climax, his seed marking me from the inside out. Then his teeth were on my shoulder, biting, but not enough to break the skin.

"Harder!" I snapped, grinding against his dick, trying to get it that last bit farther. Need burned in me, urging me to keep him inside my body and never let him leave.

"Can't," he moaned, then licked the skin over the bite mark. "You don't know what you're asking."

"Mate me," I growled back, knowing exactly what I was asking for. "Sink your teeth in my skin and claim me."

"Oh, fuck..." He cursed again, then his teeth were on my skin. I tensed, preparing for the pain, but before he could bite down, the bathroom door banged open.

Two unfamiliar wolves stood in the doorway, one on either side of Roan's younger brother. The beta's shoulders heaved as he breathed heavily. "Alpha," Micah said, his voice ragged, "there are vampires in the woods, and they're headed this way!"

Chapter Twenty-Two

Roan Silverthorne

We were as prepared for this as we could get. When we'd designed our village, we'd done so with the full knowledge that the uneasy peace we had with the leeches could end at any time.

Obviously, underground shelters hadn't been a good option here, not with the risk of flooding, but the cypress trees were thick and tall, and even better — hard to scale. Dozens of treehouses had been built, kept rustic and hidden to blend in with the tree canopy. Rope ladders usually hung down to make reaching them a breeze, but then, in times like this, they could be drawn up to prevent enemies from using them.

The number of illicit trysts we had to repeatedly break up over the past few years were proving worth it now. The young and elderly, as well as the two women near to whelping, had been ushered to safety. The rest of the wolves stood alongside me. I'd tried to convince Andy to join the young, but she'd laughed in my face.

Instead, she stood at my side, a butcher knife clutched in her steady hand. Not a hint of fear registered on her face. The way she stayed collected, radiating calm, filled me with pride. I looked at her, *really* looked, until she met my eyes with a curious tip of her head.

"When this is over, I'm going to claim you so hard," I muttered, and laughter spread through my fellow wolves. It wasn't a mean sound. Instead, it was the kind that reassured me that they'd accept her as my mate.

She smiled back, but before she could respond, a half-dozen vampires stepped out from the tree line. They formed a threatening line, despite being vastly outnumbered. I knew better than to let my guard down. I'd heard the stories — stories of a single vampire taking out scores of wolves with ease.

The king's champion might have been missing in action for centuries, but any one of these vampires could be just as dangerous, and I'd never know until it was too late.

I straightened my spine and stepped forward. "You are not welcome here. Leave, and next time you wish to visit, reach out in a civilized way." Not that I would extend an invitation if they did so, but if, by some small chance they did leave, it could buy us a few more days.

The vampires didn't move to leave. Instead, the one in the middle, a male with heavy brows, stepped forward. "Hand over the bitch, and we'll be happy to go on our way."

Fury filled me at the insult to my mate, and I growled. Before I could let my anger get away with me, though, Andromeda stepped forward, laying her hand on my arm. "Something's wrong," she said, so quiet I could barely hear her.

I turned my face slightly in her direction but refused to look away from the enemy. "What do you mean?" I asked, just as quiet.

"Arlow's not here. She should be, though. I can smell her. So...if she's not, where is she?" Andromeda frowned, her gaze scanning the surrounding forest.

I tensed, but before I could move in front of her, I heard it. A twanging sound, too quiet to pinpoint the direction. I grabbed for Andromeda at the same time the six vampires moved, so quick they seemed to blur. My wolves leapt into action.

A bolt that reeked of holly pierced the empty air where Andromeda had just been standing before I grabbed her, close enough that a chunk of her hair was severed by its steel head, fluttering to the ground. I wrapped my body around her, trusting my wolves to slow the vampires down until I got her to safety.

It wasn't necessary.

Suddenly, a streak raced toward us from the woods, long blonde hair a white-gold blur...Arlow. But before she could reach us, a second blur struck her from the side, taking her to the ground. Before I could even register what was happening, Arlow screamed. At the same time, the man who struck her fell to the side, clutching his bleeding neck.

"Shit," Andromeda cursed, voice shocked. "That's Arsenious!"

"Who?" I asked, but then the blond man groaned, tilting his face toward me.

"Andromeda," the blond man said, searching for her.

The man from my dreams...

Chapter Twenty-Three

Arsenious Dianus

I watched the woman in the metal carriage drive away, still confused by how the odd thing worked, though the woman had assured me no horses had been shrunk under the hood. Though, it did have something called 'horsepower', whatever that meant. I'd tried convincing her to drive the carriage along the wooden path.

She'd just laughed and said I was 'silly' before putting the car in park, though I had no idea what a public garden had to do with anything, to let me out. The scent was stronger here. I was definitely on the right track.

Unfortunately, I wasn't only one on that track. Her trail was overlaid with the stench of other vampires, including one that was far too familiar. The woman...the sharp-tongued blonde woman with the needles that had left my head fuzzy for so many years.

Somehow, she'd beaten me here.

I picked up the pace, tracking the scent as quickly as I could. I slowed as the scent grew stronger, unwilling to walk into an ambush. I wouldn't do anyone any good if I let myself get caught. I slunk off the path, walking silently toward what I could now see was a small, primitive village.

Lycans, I noticed, the scent thick in my nose, and I tensed. The war was over—by hundreds of years, even if it felt like only a handful to me. I had no reason to be worried. The vampires were likely a bigger threat, but old habits died hard. Even seeing the familiar redhead woman, the one whose scent drew me here, standing with the Lycans, facing off to six vampires who clearly meant her harm, wasn't enough to completely bury the antagonism.

I froze as I realized that I recognized the man standing next to the redheaded woman. He'd been in my dreams as well. The man in the room, the Protector.

And the man in the moss, the Lover.

It was destined, and just like I knew. I knew that I was meant to be his.

My distraction almost cost me everything. I hadn't even seen the blonde bitch when she fired the crossbow, my heart stopping in my chest as I watched the poison-laced dart—I could smell the stench of holly from here—flying too quick to stop toward the redhead.

Andromeda, my inner voice whispered, and horror grew even stronger. My King's daughter, barely more than a babe in arms when I'd seen her last, all grown up. Did I fail him? Dishonor the gift of immortality he bestowed on me all millennia ago by failing to save the child of his blood?

All because I was too distracted by the delicate-looking hand that she placed on the Lycan's arm.

But the Lycan moved quick as lightning, snatching her out of the bolt's path with barely inches to spare. The blonde bitch cursed and dropped the crossbow, drawing a sharp stake instead. She took off at a sprint and I followed, cutting her off from the side. I struck her with all the force I could muster. Bones shattered under me, and she screamed. She couldn't stop me from gripping her wrist and twisting, until the stake was pointed at her chest.

A quick shove and the sharp tip pierced her, violet blood spilling from the bleeding heart, cold against my skin. She was dead. As soon as it entered her flesh, she was dead, even if her body didn't recognize it yet. She scrabbled at my neck, and I cursed, letting go to clutch at the deep scratches with a bloody hand.

Should have known the bitch had claws. At least the marks were shallow, even if it meant she'd gotten her own in the end. Still, it wasn't enough to save her. Foam, brilliant yellow, spilled from her mouth as she choked, the poison hitting her system. A quick shove of the stake and she shuddered, her body going still.

I fell backward, breathing heavy. It had been too close of a call for my liking. Not for myself, for... "Andromeda," I said, turning to look for her. Had the other vampires backed off with the death of their little ringleader?

The other vampires were on their knees, their hands lifted in surrender while the Lycans worked on binding them. Andromeda was staring at me in shock, held safe in the arms of her Alpha. I sagged in relief, watching her like a hawk as she ran toward me.

"Arsenious?" she cried, her voice shaking. I was surprised she recognized me, grown as she was, but the way her eyes met mine, the fear that filled them... I suspected that it was not the first time she'd seen me.

"Andromeda?" I rasped, scanning her for injuries I may have missed. She looked...perfect.

"Are you...? Is it really you? Are you sane?" she asked, hesitating until I nodded. Then, she dropped to her knees, not seeming to care about the mud that marked her jeans.

"Princess!" I scrambled to my feet, reaching out to pull her up before I froze, unwilling to mar her perfection with bloody hands. Instead, I turned to the Alpha with pleading eyes, "Help her," I asked, the words echoing my earlier dream.

His eyes sharpened at the words, and something told me that he had dreamed it as well. *A true dream, then.*

"I don't need help, but clearly *you* do," Andromeda snapped, pushing herself to her feet and gripping my chin, tipping to the side to stare at my neck.

"'Tis but a scratch, Princess," I promised, touched by her worry.

Then she let go of my chin to slap my cheek, and I felt a bit less touched. "Don't call me that, Arsen. Call me Andy. You fucker, you scared the shit out of me. Do you know how pissed Father would be if anything happened to you?"

Still, there was a flush to her cheeks as her gaze met mine, and I smirked. "Just your father, *Kitten*?" I purposefully repeated the nickname from the waking dream, wondering if she'd had it, too.

When her blush darkened, I knew she had.

"What is happening?" The Alpha groaned, staring between me and the princess.

I knew the answer, knew it with the same surety I knew that the sun would be rising in the morning. I'd seen it before, in the ages prior to the Lycan Uprisings. Whenever our species bonded, it started with the

Dreaming. Of course, such matings had grown rare, even before my drugged stupor.

"We're your mates, Alpha."

Chapter Twenty-Four

Roan Silverthorne

"Mates?" I repeated, breath rapidly increasing. Part of me had suspected it as soon as I recognized him as the man from my dreams. My wolf howled his agreement inside me. "Mates," I said again, though this time it was not a question.

"Alpha," said the vampire. I recognized him now, up close as he was. This was the King's Champion, the vampire who had slaughtered hundreds, if not thousands of my kind during the Revolution — the vampire whose name I'd never learned because survivors had been too terrified to speak it.

And he called me Alpha with such submissiveness…

It had my dick plumping in my jeans.

He kept speaking as if he didn't notice, though his gaze dropped to my erection and held. "With the blonde bitch dead, the princess — I'm sorry," he corrected himself when Andromeda hissed at him.

"Andy will need to return to the Sanctuary, at least until the king can verify she's safe. I'm sure he must be worried."

Andromeda flinched. "Arsenious, my father has been given to the earth for healing. It will be weeks before he rises."

Arsenious went still, his face blank as a mask, then he nodded. Still, I don't think I imagined the pain in his eyes, the way the skin tightened around them for a moment. "We have some time, then."

Andy looked at me with doe eyes. "He needs a shower, and I think we could all use a place to rest with a *real* bed. Besides, I don't think it would be a good idea to keep *them*" — she gestured to the bound vampires — "here for very long."

I sighed, knowing she was right but unwilling to let the pair of vampires leave without me, not now that I knew they belonged to me. Part of me longed to stay here, in the pack I had built by hand. But there were more important things than what I wanted.

They were right. They needed to go back, and it *wasn't* safe to keep the leeches here. Any one of them could break free and take out half the pack — slaughter our pups and women in their sleep…in a heartbeat.

"Micah," I called, searching out my brother with my gaze. His eyes were serious when they met mine. "Keep the pack safe while we're gone," I ordered, though it came out more a plea.

"On my life, Brother," he promised.

I turned back to Andromeda and Arsenious. "We'll go to the Sanctuary." They both looked relieved, though even they couldn't hide their nerves at the thought of returning.

The boats were cramped and uncomfortable, and I spent the entire trip on the water on the edge of terror, not just that the vampires would break free somehow and leave us for dead—though it was a concern—but that any one of the nighttime dangers would cause us to sink before I could prevent it. Likely, we'd survive, but I didn't relish the thought of trying to navigate the swamp on foot, not this deep in the bayou and especially not with prisoners.

Thankfully, we made it safely to the marina and into the vehicles—or the 'metal monsters' as Arsenious kept calling them. Despite the late hour—though it was probably early for the vampires, creatures of the night that they were—New Orleans was bustling. People said New York was the city that never slept, but I thought they had it wrong.

New Orleans was a city of parties and night life. Anyone who'd ever been to Mardi Gras could attest to it.

The Sanctuary was like an oasis of calm. A pair of guards opened the gate just far enough for one to step out and approach the window of the rusty truck, gesturing for me to roll it down.

"State your business," the vampire said, clearly put out at the thought of letting a wolf through the gates.

Andromeda leaned around me and the vampire went even paler at the sight. "Princess! The king has been beside himself with worry."

"My father? He's awake?" Andromeda sounded shocked, but to be fair, so was I. She'd said it would take another week at least.

"The fae delegation woke him," the guard explained, then waved frantically at the gates until they started opening. "Go on through. I swear, he's got the thralls so scared they're thinking of leaving. Best you go straight to the throne room."

"Stubborn man should be resting," Andy replied, exasperation in her voice, but then she grinned. "We have a surprise for him. It should put him in a *great* mood. Oh, I need some guards to escort the traitors tied up in the back of the van behind us down to the cells until father decides what to do with them."

"Traitors?" the guard yelped, glancing at the vehicle that was idling behind us.

"They and Low tried to kill me. Lucky for me, Arsenious was there," Andy explained, and the guard she was speaking to looked even more shocked.

Arsenious had chosen to sit in the back, farther from the 'angry horses' under the hood. Andromeda had explained to me that he had been stuck in something called bloodlust for over two hundred years, kept locked up in a special cell in the dungeons the whole time.

He was acclimating better than I expected, all things considered. The world had changed a lot in that time.

"Arsenious is awake?" the guard breathed, trying to peer around us. "Go on through, quick. The king will be so pleased."

I glanced back at Arsen, who had a soft smile on his face at the mention of his sire. "I look forward to seeing him again," Arsen murmured. "I only hope he is not angry with me."

"He never gave up hoping you'd return to us," Andy answered, reassuring him.

"I wish we'd had time to clean up," I bemoaned as we left the cars behind — after carefully watching the traitors be escorted inside to make sure none escaped — and headed in ourselves. The Vampire King had been snooty enough during our last visit, and now here we were showing up covered in dirt and blood. And unlike last time, where the only thing on the line was a distribution deal, now I had my mates to worry about.

I swallowed, anxious at the thought of telling him that I was planning on claiming not one but both of his heirs as my mates. I didn't plan on asking for permission. I was simply doing him the courtesy of giving him notice.

Soon, we would have to sit down together and work out how our relationship would look. They had duties here, and I couldn't abandon my pack. *Maybe we should set up a schedule?*

I was still musing on the logistics when Andromeda leaned up on her toes and kissed me, distracting me from my thoughts. "Come on, Alpha. Once my father understands the situation, he won't care about a bit of mud."

"No, I think he'll be too busy trying to remove my head from my body," I muttered darkly, but the very real possibility that the Vampire King would be feeling murderous wasn't enough to stop me from following Andy, unannounced, into the throne room.

Chapter Twenty-Five

Andromeda Dianus

"That went well," Arsenious said, beaming brightly as we left the throne room and started up the stairs to my tower.

Both Roan and I stopped to stare at him. "If you think that went *well*, I'd hate to see what you consider poorly..." Roan said dryly.

I couldn't say I disagreed. "I suppose we left with all our appendages..." I mused, though that was the bare minimum expectation. I wasn't sure I'd ever seen my father's face get so purple before.

And it wasn't even Arlow's death he was pissed about—though I could tell he felt her absence. If he'd truly cared for her, her death would have been devastating. For years after my mother passed, he'd been little more than a shade. Now, though, he was annoyed at best. Even that amount of emotion seemed to stem more from having to track down and cancel her subscriptions and credit cards.

He'd been so much more pissed at the thought of having a 'stinking dog' as a son-in-law someday.

As soon as I'd threatened to move to the pack lands full time, though, he'd calmed down — even if he did keep glaring at Roan like he hoped his head would explode if he tried hard enough. He'd cooled down a little bit when Roan had agreed we could live at least part time at the Sanctuary *and* that, considering the situation, he'd be willing to renegotiate the terms of their distribution deal.

"Your dad is kind of scary," Roan said with a shudder, but his eyes betrayed him.

"You *like* him." I grinned.

"I can't help it. He might be pissed, but I respect that he worries for you," Roan admitted, and he sounded so begrudging that I couldn't help but laugh.

"Don't worry," I said as we reached the top of the staircase. I could hardly wait until we got into my rooms to back the Alpha wolf against the wall. I ran a finger down the buttons of his shirt. "We'll protect you from my daddy. Won't we, Arsen?" I turned slightly to smirk at the older vampire, who was watching my fingers move on Roan's shirt with a hungry look.

"Yes, Alpha," he agreed, though I suspected he was only half listening.

After nearly three hundred or so years of celibacy, I couldn't blame him for being distracted.

"See?" I smirked up at Roan. "Nothing to be scared of."

Suddenly, Roan grabbed my wrists and used the grip to spin us around. Now it was my back against the wall, and I was trapped by his larger body. His eyes were dark with lust and full of promise as he held me in place. "I'm not scared, Kitten, but *you* should be." He grinned. "There's two of us now... Think you can handle us both?"

I looked between him and Arsen. "Oh, I can handle you. The real question is whether *you* can handle *me.*"

"Challenge accepted..." Roan growled and yanked my arms over my head, pinning me against the wall. Then, his mouth was on mine, his kiss demanding. He pulled away just long enough to order Arsen over.

"Get her pants off," Roan said, then his mouth was on mine again. Arsen's hands were steady as he worked open the button of my jeans and lowered the zipper. It didn't take long for him to have me bare from the waist down. My pants had barely hit the floor, kicked away along with my shoes, before Roan was yanking my shirt over my head to join them.

There was something obscenely erotic about standing nude while both of them were fully dressed. Then Roan said, "On your knees, Kitten. I want to watch you make Arsen feel good. He deserves it, doesn't he? Go on... Tell him thank you for saving your life like a good girl."

Every inch of me went hot as I dropped to my knees with a whimper. And Arsen had his dick out, though I hadn't seen him open his pants. Was he that fast, or was I that excited?

His dick was beautiful, not something I usually thought about them, if I were honest. But his was practically perfect. A bit longer than Alpha's and on the thinner side, with just the right curve to it.

And he was already leaking pre-cum. Alpha moved to stand behind Arsen. He was slightly taller, giving him the perfect vantage point to look down on me over

Arsen's shoulder. "Look at her. See how hungry she is for it?" Alpha said quietly enough that I barely heard him, though Arsen shuddered. Then, Roan wrapped his arm around the older vampire's waist, gripping his dick and guiding it toward my mouth.

Alpha ran the crown along my tongue, coating it in the sticky pre-cum. Arsen tasted of salt and cherries, sweeter than Alpha but not necessarily better. They were different, but I didn't think it would be possible for me to choose a favorite.

I whined as Alpha gripped my chin, forcing my mouth open farther. "Go on, Arsen. Use her mouth. If she wants you to stop, she'll tap your thigh twice." Alpha met my eyes. "Won't you, Kitten?"

I nodded my head as best I could. I had no intentions of either of them stopping.

Arsen slid his dick back into my mouth, letting it rest heavy on my tongue for a second, but then he groaned and started to move, thrusting in and out faster than I could swallow. His pre-cum mixed with my saliva and trailed down my chin.

"Look at you, making a mess," Alpha mumbled, but his voice was proud, an expression full of approval. Heat flooded my body when, after a particularly rough thrust that had me gagging, Alpha rewarded the sound by angling Arsen's head back and kissing him. From my knees, I had the perfect view of it.

Their mouths lingered together, tongues dancing, and the sight had me clenching my thighs together and moaning. The sound was enough to get their attention, though, and they broke apart, both of them staring down at me with heat in their eyes.

"I think she likes watching," Alpha said, giving me an evil grin. He flattened his left hand against Arsen's belly, the other reaching around to guide his dick out of my mouth.

"Please," I begged, leaning forward in an attempt to keep tasting him.

Alpha chuckled. "Be good, Kitten. I don't want him coming until he's in that tight pussy of yours. Get on the bed."

I scrambled to obey, almost running into my bedroom to clamber on top of my king-sized mattress. It shocked me how close I felt to the pair of men, considering we'd practically just met, but I felt like I'd known them my whole life.

I lay down on my back, hands over my head with one knee propped up, displaying my body to its best advantage. Roan and Arsen took longer to follow, but I realized why as soon as they entered. They were both beautifully, *gloriously* naked, their dicks pointing toward me like a compass.

Arsen's hands were empty, but Alpha was carrying a few travel packets of lube. He tossed them onto the mattress beside me. "Lie down, Arsen," Roan ordered, then Arsen was scrambling up beside me to lie down on his back.

This wasn't the vampire of the legends—the strong champion who took no prisoners and showed no mercy. Part of me wondered if time had changed him, the centuries of bloodlust leaving him so needy that he was willing to cave to Alpha if it meant getting laid.

But then I met his gaze, and he looked so earnest that I knew that wasn't it. Maybe in the past, he'd been a cold-blooded killer. Maybe that person still lived inside him…but this Arsen, this sweetly submissive man? This Arsen was just as real.

"Can you take him without prep?" Alpha asked, climbing gracefully on the bed and kneeling, watching us both with the confidence of a king.

"Yes, Alpha," I panted, wanting it, *needing* it. I'd have taken them both at once, at this point, if it meant not being so empty.

"Then show me what a good girl you are," Alpha ordered. "Don't come, though."

I groaned, nodding, even if I wasn't sure I was going to be able to hold out. My pussy was already soaked, just from the brief blow job, and Arsen looked ready to blow as well. His dick was hard and purple at the head, looking nearly as wet as I was.

I swung a leg over his hips before reaching down to grip that perfectly shaped dick, lining the head up with my slit. I lowered myself slowly, afraid I'd come if I moved any faster, but far too soon he was fully sheathed, long enough to stroke every inch of my channel with hardly any effort.

Arsen moaned, his hands large on my hips as he held me in place. I watched him clench his eyes closed, his teeth gritted, and endorphins flooded me at the sight. I loved knowing that I was doing this to him. That *I* was the cause of this perfect agony.

Then it was my turn to moan as a lube-slick finger brushed over my ass without warning, pushing inside in a smooth motion that somehow managed not to burn. "Oh God," I cried, falling forward. My hands landed on Arsen's firm chest, leaving my ass even more open to Alpha's tender ministrations as he worked me open — first one finger, then two, then three.

Then, finally, I felt the head of his dick against my hole, wet with lube, and he was pushing inside. "Fuck!"

I screamed, the stretch unbearable…but in the best way.

"So tight, Kitten," Alpha groaned as he seated himself fully. "I can feel Arsen in your pussy, stretching you out. Doing so good, taking both our dicks…."

He held steady, letting me adjust, and Arsen tried. He couldn't seem to help the little twitches of his hips or the way his hands clenched, pulling me that last little bit closer. Each small movement felt infinitely larger, but it was me who finally broke, shifting my hips in an effort to get some form of friction.

Our groans joined together in a symphony of pleasure. Alpha rested his hands over Arsen's and the two of them moved together, sliding in and out, in and out in a perfect harmony, fucking me until sweat clung to each of us, and I felt boneless.

"Bite me, Alpha!" I cried, opening my neck to his teeth. "Please, claim us…"

The words must have been enough to push him over, because Alpha Roan groaned, then his teeth were in my shoulder, clamping down in the bonding bite. Ecstasy filled me. As soon as his hips stuttered and he released my shoulder, I fell forward and sank *my* teeth into Arsen. Whether it was the change in position or the taste of his blood, it was enough to tip me over, then I was coming, too, my pussy and asshole clenching on their hard dicks.

Alpha cursed, pulling out of my ass, and I felt his seed leaking out onto my skin, but Arsen stayed deep inside me, groaning as he started to spill. As soon as I freed my teeth, he leaned forward and sank *his* fangs into the other side of my neck, adding his mark to my skin.

The three of us collapsed, sated, into a boneless heap.

I was nearly asleep when I felt Roan get out of bed. I yawned and propped myself up on an elbow. "Where are you sneaking off to?" I asked, but he lifted a finger to his lips. Then, he pointed behind me, toward Arsen.

The handsome vampire was still on his back, but his mouth was open, soft snores spilling from between his reddened lips. He didn't seem to mind the cum drying to his skin. I grimaced, though, realizing how sticky I felt.

"Bathroom?" Alpha asked quietly.

"What if I said it was outside?" I whispered, but I pointed toward the attached en suite with a grin.

Roan rolled his eyes, but he smiled as well, returning a moment later with a damp cloth. He wiped me clean with gentle hands, then he wiped Arsen as well, even lifting his balls to clean beneath them.

Arsen slept through it all, which, I thought as a yawn split my lips, was a good idea. It was nearing dawn and I hadn't slept since... God, was it only the day before yesterday? It seemed unbelievable that so much had happened in so little time. But I realized as I snuggled down between Roan and Arsenious...I wouldn't have it any other way.

Our relationship might just be beginning, but something inside me knew that somehow, everything was all going to work out. I could see us together a hundred years from now — a thousand — growing old together, or the closest thing to it that our kind came.

I could see Roan horseplaying around with a litter of our children, and Arsenious kissing their scuffed knees and bruised elbows.

"You're thinking too much, Kitten," Roan said, brushing his lips over my forehead. "Go to sleep. It'll all be here in the morning."

"Yes, Alpha."

Epilogue

Roan Silverthorne
Ten years later

"Giddyap, Daddy!" my son Remy said between giggles, kicking his heels into my sides and tightening his tiny arms around my neck. I choked, quickly slipping a few fingers beneath his arms to loosen them, then hiked him farther up my back. He might be small, but he was a strong little rascal. "Faster, faster!"

"No, no faster!" James—Remy's most timid littermate—cried, his grip on my left thigh tightening. Their sister, Kallie, was a lead weight on my right leg.

"Papa soon," Kallie promised, and when I looked down for a quick second, her reassuring smile was all I saw, so like her mother's.

Speaking of her mother, Andromeda's voice sounded from down the hall. "*There* you all are. I swear I've searched the whole place twice!"

I hated being away from my mates, but sometimes, vampire business made their absence unavoidable. Thankfully, this time it had been a short trip to the city. I'd taken the pups in to see their grandfather, then we'd be heading back to the bayou. The city was too busy and too bustling with people for my comfort, and even after a decade, Arsenious hadn't quite gotten used to the way time had changed things.

He'd never admit it — he wasn't built that way — but he wasn't the same unshakable champion he'd been before the king's mistress had drugged him into bloodlust. He was softer around the edges, with a vulnerability that made me want to keep him wrapped in cotton and bubble wrap.

Or, better yet, in the sheets of my bed.

I knew Andy sensed it to. There was a reason she tried as much as possible to keep her visits to the city to a minimum. Neither of us wanted to see Arsenious struggling.

"Hey, Kitten," I purred, wrapping my free arm around her back and pulling her close. "Miss me?"

"Eeew," Remy groaned into my ear. "No! No gross time!"

"Tell your children to close their eyes" — I grinned down at her — "because I plan on kissing you now."

"Yuck!" James groaned and buried his face against my leg.

I didn't wait for her to warn them, since I was mostly just teasing. The pups were still at the age they found kissing 'gross', which meant even surrounded by them as we were, we'd still have some privacy.

I leaned down and pressed my lips to hers. They softened immediately, giving way to my tongue and opening. We might have only been apart for two days, but even that was too much for me. I wanted to take her in my arms and keep her there forever — to just enjoy the way she melted for me.

But our family wouldn't be complete until we saw Arsenious. I sighed as we broke apart. "Are they still in a meeting?"

Andy grimaced. "Dad didn't have a problem with the new label design, but..."

"Let me guess, Caelon doesn't approve," I finished, not surprised. "Should we go rescue Arsen?" I gestured to the throne room. The wards had strong enough sound dampeners that I couldn't hear *what* was being said, but I could hear the raised voices.

"Probably for the best," Andy agreed, scooping up Kallie and resting the toddler on her hips. At eight, the pups had finally learned to walk, but that meant we spent more time chasing after them than heading in the right direction. Back at home, we let them be as free range as possible. Here at the Sanctuary, they tended to end up in one of our arms more often than not.

The vampire enforcer at the door to the throne room reached out to Remy, pretending to steal his nose until the boy giggled, before he held the door for us.

The argument going on inside broke off abruptly as we entered. King Dianus stood from the plush maroon armchair he called a throne, throwing his arms out wide. "My grandbabies!"

James tumbled off my leg as he let go, off balance as he hurried toward the king. "Me down, me down!" Remy whined, struggling to squirm down on his own. I helped lower him to his feet, grinning as he toddled after his brother.

Kallie was the only one of our pups who didn't fight to be put down — mostly because she wasn't the strongest walker yet. She just blinked at her mama who, like me, had a hard time saying no to her.

Andy carried her closer, passing her over to my father-in-law. King Dianus cooed at her as he took her, rubbing the tips of their noses together in their special butterfly kiss.

Even Caelon smiled at the pups, though he looked a bit pained. "We can discuss the appropriate color scheme at a later time, I suppose. There are still a few weeks until they need to go to print."

When we'd asked the Collective for help, we'd assumed they'd send a cloaked representative — someone old, serious and powerful, who would show up, set things to right then disappear.

We hadn't expected the naked fae boy...and we *certainly* hadn't expected him to stick around. After he'd kicked Arlow from the Sanctuary and woken the king from the earth, they'd taken one look at each other and fallen in lust. Love did, eventually, come as well. For the most part, having a fae twink lingering around didn't change much except the interior decorating.

Caelon had very particular ideas about design, though, which only really became a problem when the Silverthorne Moonshine company decided to rebrand. This was the second time we'd done so since he'd arrived, and both times had been...interesting.

I, personally, didn't really care what the bottles looked like. As long as the contents tasted good and the price stayed low enough the average person could buy it, that was really all that mattered.

Andromeda didn't care, either. As soon as she'd found the grimoire that I'd bought out of spite during that first, fated trip to the city, she'd gotten so wrapped up in practicing the new spells and potions that I frequently had to remind her to eat in the first place. After a few years, her obsession had lessened a bit, but the brewery was still barely on her radar. Between witchcraft and the kids, she had her own priorities.

Arsenious, though…

He'd taken to the business end of things like a fish to water. He and Caelon had come to heads often enough that I was *minorly* afraid that one of these days, they'd end up killing each other over something as silly as font size.

But hey, what was family without a little drama?

I waited until Arsenious met my gaze, then winked. He flushed, his skin burning violet, and I knew that later tonight, after the pups were put to bed for the third and final time, he would come to my bed and kneel for me.

And after that, when all three of us were sated, lying in each other's arms, I knew we'd be just as much in love as we had been ten years ago — the first time we'd come together in this tower.

Just like I knew that in another ten years, I'd feel this very same way.

Want to see more like this?
Here's a taster for you to enjoy!

Hot Bite: Under the Sun and Sky
AE Lister

Excerpt

There were days that I regretted ever becoming Joanna Kilkenny. Those days had outnumbered the other ones for a long time now. Tonight, the premiere of *Lowlife*, my latest film, was being held at the Meridian Arts Centre in Toronto, and it was the last place I wanted to be.

In my room at the Ritz-Carlton hotel, I stared at my reflection in the mirror as my assistant put the finishing touches to my updo. We'd kept it simple, but I had a hell of a lot of hair.

"Thank you, Nadine. That's perfect."

She smiled at me in the mirror. "You're welcome, Joanna. Have a wonderful evening."

I watched her gather her things and leave, while a text from Jamie came through on my phone.

The car is here.

I smiled and sent a reply.

I'll be there shortly. Nadine is just leaving.

Jamie sent a thumbs-up emoji.

* * * *

The lights were blinding as I made my way from the limo through a crowd of excited paparazzi, with Jamie at my elbow.

"Holy fuck," he muttered. "It's worse every time."

"Or better?" I replied, trying to access the part of me that still cared about my popularity.

Jamie grunted. "They'll be trying to tear a piece off you next."

Hmm. That would be interesting. I'd like to see someone try.

Jamie Conrad, my ruggedly handsome bodyguard, spoke with a compelling Irish brogue that only added to his appeal.

I grinned at him. "Not with you on duty," I said, confident in Jamie's ability to keep me safe. Although, in truth, I didn't need a protector—only a shield between me and the public who thought I was one thing when I was actually something else. Keeping my true identity a secret would have been difficult if I'd needed to exert my strength on more than rare occasions.

My name had been Alba de Gradi for more than two hundred years, but I'd gone by Joanna Kilkenny for the past twenty-five.

Joanna Kilkenny, award-winning actor known for roles in outstanding film noir and mystery cinema. I was a sparkling jewel in the Hollywood crown—a role I'd played with aplomb and delight for those first ten years.

It was getting a little old...and so was I. At least, people were beginning to wonder why I didn't look as old as I was *supposed* to be.

At the start of my Hollywood career, I had pretended to be an inexperienced twenty-six-year-old ingénue. For anyone watching — which now included a vast number of devoted fans, most of the press and many, many others — I should have been in my early fifties.

The fact that I continued to look the same as when I'd started was regarded with awe and commendation from many, but with more and more suspicion from a few. There were people who probably knew what I was. And as the years went on, it would become more and more difficult to pretend to be human.

I'd needed an exit strategy. And tonight's non-appearance at the international premiere for *Lowlife* would be the first phase of my escape from public life in America.

Once inside the Meridian, I was relieved to be out of sight of all the chaos.

"Ms. Kilkenny?" a nervous intern said. "May I show you to your room?"

"Thank you, yes," I responded, looking him over. He was young, with a swimmer's body, but I tamped down my blood and other lusts and smiled. "What's your name?"

The young man blinked, and his cheeks flushed. "Uh, it's Casper."

"I'm pleased to meet you, Casper." I could already see that he had fallen under my spell. Even beyond my substantial supernatural gifts, the ability to charm the pants off people — both figuratively and literally — was a power I wielded with abandon.

"Let's go," Jamie said, placing his familiar hand at the small of my back and causing a pleasant tingle in my spine as he did so. *Ever the practical one.*

I followed Casper, my Louboutin heels clicking on the tile as he led us down a bright hallway past other interns and people working the event who cast wide-eyed glances my way and spoke to each other in hushed voices. I tried not to notice the tight curves of Casper's ass in his pressed black pants, but it was hopeless. I'd always been partial to men's asses. That would never change, no matter how many centuries I endured. Men's rear ends and other parts were some of the things that made immortality worth it.

If I didn't have solid plans for the brief amount of time I'd spend in this building, I'd have made sure to give Casper my card with an invitation to join me in the privacy of my rooms for a short dalliance — something that Jamie would roll his pretty eyes at but then stand outside my door and try not to listen to.

I knew of Jamie's regard for me, feelings he tried to hide in the interests of professional detachment and a sense of unfounded inferiority. He was more than my bodyguard and he knew it, but so far we'd only traversed the bounds of friendship. I knew he wanted more and was too afraid to show it — or ask for it.

Which amused me, as I would give him anything he asked for in an instant. He didn't know it yet, just like he wasn't aware of my true nature or any of my plans with Lorne, but I hoped he cared enough about me to be a pivotal part of my exodus. I'd know by the end of the night. And he would have to decide whether he wanted me and all that involved or a life of work and drudgery in the celebrity trenches of twenty-first-century California.

Speaking of which, I needed to see if my VIP guest had arrived.

"Casper, do you know if Lorne Dechenes is here yet?" I asked as we moved along.

In my peripheral vision, I saw Jamie's head jerk to the side as he threw a startled glance my way. Jamie Conrad didn't like to be surprised. He prided himself on being ready for anything. but he couldn't possibly be prepared for what was going down tonight.

"He's already in your room, Ms. Kilkenny."

Perfect. Everything was going ahead as we'd arranged it.

"What the fuck?" Jamie said. He'd moved in close enough to whisper in my ear.

I waved a hand in the air. "He's an old friend."

"He's your ex-lover. He's a famous rock star. What the fuck is he doing *here*?"

We were still walking, following Casper. The hallway seemed endless, but I knew my room was near the exit to the back parking lot. It always was. We came in through the front and left through the back, like all sensible Hollywood celebrities.

"He's coming to see me, of course. Don't be jealous. I'd love to introduce you."

"Hmm. Do I want to meet 'America's Brattiest Rock-Star'? I'm not really sure I do."

"Don't be silly. Lorne is wonderful."

"Then why did you break up with him?"

I shrugged. "It's complicated."

"It always is with you, Joanna."

Oh, you sweet, sweet man. You have no idea.

"Here we are," Casper said, stopping at a green door marked with the number twenty, which had my name in a silver holder.

Joanna Kilkenny.

It was a pretty name that rolled off the tongue, and probably the only thing I'd miss.

I stopped and let Jamie go ahead of me. He rapped on the door once then twisted the handle, pushing it open.

"Lorne," he said, in acknowledgment of the leather-clad man sprawled on a black velvet sofa with a drink in his hand.

"Jamie Conrad! Still guarding the precious jewel?"

"It's my job, yeah."

He ushered me in and began a quick walk-around the space as Lorne stood and stepped toward me.

"Baby," Lorne said, his eyes brimming with emotion.

"Fuck, you look amazing. I've missed you!" My dead heart fluttered at the sight of him.

When you'd been around as long as I had, you put a lot of value on people who gave you joy and relationships that withstood the test of time. We'd broken up solely as a necessity, in order to hatch the plan that was coming to fruition at this moment.

Lorne raised his eyebrows in a silent request. I inclined my chin and he moved sinuously into my open arms. I pulled him against me, feeling the familiar curves and angles of his body as if they were a beloved landscape.

"Fuck. I've missed *you*," he breathed into my ear.

I gazed over his shoulder at Jamie, who had finished his safety circuit and now stood staring. When I winked, he moved his gaze away and cleared his throat.

"Everything looks good. I'll be outside."

"Thank you, Jamie," I said, before I latched onto Lorne's seeking mouth. The door clicked shut as Lorne groaned and all the passion I'd sequestered away slammed back into my body.

"Goddammit," Lorne muttered against my lips, his breaths ragged, his mouth desperate, his tongue seeking mine.

I responded to his desperation with my own. He tasted the same. No…better. The scent of his blood was dizzying.

Finally, he pulled back and devoured my face with his gaze as eagerly as his tongue had plundered my mouth.

"Hungry?" he asked.

I gave a breathless laugh, clutching at his wiry arms in the leather jacket, and nodded. "Always."

Lorne melted against me and turned his head, moving the collar of his jacket aside and offering his pale neck. At the scent of his familiar blood, I closed my eyes and moaned.

"Fuck." The word was barely a whisper from my lips. I shuddered, the anticipation exquisite.

Taking my time now that he was in my arms again, I licked a line from the base of his throat to just under his ear before my fangs descended and I pierced the delicate skin there.

Lorne gasped as his blood flooded my mouth. I'd waited so long for this. I closed my eyes and took a bit more, then swiped the wound closed with my tongue.

"Thank you," I murmured.

"Always," he said, turning back and capturing my lips with his. He kissed me deeply, tasting his own blood, his cock hard under his jeans.

I couldn't help smiling against his mouth.

"You're here," I said, hardly believing that he had made good on his promise. I'm not sure what I'd expected, but it became clear that I'd doubted him.

He sighed and pulled back, giving me a closed-mouthed kiss on the corner of my lips, as if he regretted having to stop. "Joanna…"

I frowned. "You know my real name."

"*Alba. Joanna.* It doesn't matter to me."

"It matters to me, Lorne. From now on, it's Alba."

"All right. All right."

I nodded, assuaged. "Come. Sit down. I need to talk to you about something."

"All right." *My obedient rock-star lover.*

He took my hand and led me to the sofa, where we sat side-by-side, his eyes fixed on me as if he could hardly believe I was real.

"Is everything ready?" I asked.

Lorne grinned. "Everything's arranged. The plane is waiting for us at Buttonville."

Buttonville Airfield was a small airport for private and chartered planes out of Toronto.

"And Villa Del Cielo?" I asked, eager for his reassurance that we were leaving and had a place waiting for us, just as we had discussed so many years ago.

"Don't worry, Alba. Everything is prepared, just as you wanted."

"So we can disappear?" I asked, hardly believing the time had finally come.

About the Author

Kady Ellis loves women—in all shapes and sizes. They write across the romance spectrum, but all their books have one thing in common: a happily ever after (eventually). If you're seeking men loving men, consider the works they've published under their other penname, KD Ellis. She/they.

Kady loves to hear from readers. You can find their contact information, website details and author profile page at https://www.totallybound.com

Home of Erotic Romance

Sign up for our newsletter and find out about all our romance book releases, eBook sales and promotions, sneak peeks and FREE romance books!